Fling With The Flying Doctor

Kathleen Ryder

DEDICATION

For Wyatt, with love.

CHAPTER ONE

"Can you hear that?" Meghan addressed the driver, breathing an inward sigh of relief as she heard the aircraft approaching overhead. Finally! "That will be the Royal Flying Doctor Service, as soon as they land, we will have you out of here." Meghan had hardly dared to leave the driver for any longer than a few moments at a time and had hurriedly dashed back and forth between the crashed car and the reflective safety poles by the side of the road for the past ten minutes, knocking down as many as she possibly could. It wouldn't be enough, she knew that, the pilot would have to do the rest as he taxied towards them. Meghan held her breath as she watched the pilot line the plane up with the highway perfectly, before descending and screaming towards them. For one heart-stopping moment, Meghan wondered if the pilot would stop in time, and instinctively threw herself protectively across the body of the driver. The aircraft came to a standstill with less than a metre to spare, the stairs dropping down before the propellers had even stopped, the two occupants descending the stairs and sprinting forwards towards the car and Meghan.

Extricating herself from the front of the car, Meghan started speaking as soon as they were within earshot. "I was the one who called it in, there were no other cars on the scene when I arrived. Single passenger, male, 63, his driver's licence says his name is Robert Frost. He has abdominal swelling, has been in and out of consciousness, and his heart rate is one hundred and thirty beats per minute, suspected tachycardia," Meghan fell silent as she watched vitals being checked and recorded, equipment changing hands at lightning speed. It was obvious to her that these two worked seamlessly as a team. With a heart monitor and intravenous drip attached, the driver was finally freed from his car and transferred to a stretcher.

"Here," Meghan gathered up his personal effects and stashed them in a plastic bag, placing them on the stretcher near his legs. "Will he be okay?"

"It was a good call," piercing blue eyes met hers questioningly, "doctor?"

"I'm a nurse, Meghan Richards."

"Doctor James Cristo," he nodded, "and my flight nurse, Samantha Ryan."

With Robert Frost secured inside the aircraft, Meghan helped the others manually turn the Royal Flying Doctor Service plane around, the highway being too narrow for it to turn without assistance. With a nod in her direction, James was gone, leaving Meghan to stare at his retreating back. She watched from the safety of her car as the Royal Flying Doctor Service plane took off, tracking it with her eyes across the endless blue of the outback sky until it glimmered and disappeared. As she started her car and headed for Alice Springs, she was surprised to find herself smiling.

CHAPTER TWO

Meghan squared her shoulders and took a deep breath, opening the door gently and stepping into the darkened room. A quick check of the clipboard on the end of the bed confirmed what Meghan already knew, Ben had suffered a rough night. Meghan moved to his bed and took his observations as carefully as she could, loathe to wake him or his tired mother currently napping in the chair next to his bed. Ben had been Meghan's patient for several weeks now, originally coming in due to a broken leg sustained during a fall in the playground. The x-ray had shown multiple fractures and more worryingly, a shadow that couldn't be explained. Doctors had operated and repaired the break, but a subsequent biopsy had revealed the worst, little Ben had bone cancer. Ben's only chance of survival lay in finding a bone marrow donor, unfortunately, their search so far had failed to find a suitable donor. As much as Meghan tried to stay positive for Ben and his mother, she knew better than anyone that his time was fast running out.

"Meghan," Sue flung open the door, light spilling into the room, rousing Ben's mum Sarah. "They have a possible donor in Melbourne, the retrieval team is on their way, you need to get Ben ready to go, now!" Sarah burst into tears, jumping up and hugging Meghan tightly, before turning to wake Ben. Even in his disorientated state, he managed a weak smile as Meghan started disconnecting his tubes ready for transport. Sue fluttered around the room gathering up Ben's personal effects as she went, passing them to Sarah to pack in their travel case. Meghan was just bundling her notes together when a flurry of doctors entered the room. Meghan stayed with Sarah and Ben for as long as she could, knowing that Sarah had no family to help, making this trip even more difficult, and she was quick to explain anything that Sarah was unsure of. With the retrieval team ready, Meghan hugged both Sarah and Ben one last time and stepped back to watch as they were whisked off down the hallway to the waiting ambulance. There was nothing more that could be done except to wait.

Meghan had been on edge for the remainder of the day, knowing that it could be several days yet until they knew for sure if the possible donor was an actual match for Ben or not. When Sue had pleaded with Meghan to go with her to the hospital benefit tonight, catching her at a weak moment, Meghan had said yes, too tired to argue. The hospital benefit had become rather infamous around the hospital for being a loud, catty occasion where staff would drink way too much alcohol before complaining about other staff who had apparently wronged them at some point during the last millennia. As Meghan didn't drink alcohol, a major pastime of the residents of Alice Springs, and she certainly wasn't a catty gossip, she tended to avoid the hospital benefit, yet another social situation where she felt awkwardly out of place.

Meghan smiled as she caught sight of the heavily decorated Gillen Club foyer, the potted artificial palm trees arranged on top of a pile of sand and the iridescent pink plastic flamingos standing in the wading pool certainly made a statement. Meghan signed in and walked through the club to the main function room. Spotting Sue sitting at a table with their colleagues, she moved towards them, carefully manoeuvring around other party-goers and squeezing between tables. Settling down into the empty seat next to Sue, Meghan called out a hello to her co-workers before pulling a bottle of water out of her handbag and taking a large swig, leaning back in her chair and casually observing her colleagues.

There was Margaret, the eldest, and the longest-serving nurse on the children's ward. After nearly thirty years of service she had gained quite a reputation for her no-nonsense approach, she had the skill of displaying an open manner, which belied her true nature. Meghan had learnt the hard way that she needed to be exceptionally careful with what she said to Margaret unless she wanted it twisted around and passed on to the rest of the hospital staff. Seated next to Margaret was

Pearl, the youngest, and newest, member of the team, having only just started her rotation with the ward. Meghan thought that Pearl had the potential to become a great nurse if she learnt to take direction from her peers. Which just left Joanna and Erica sitting at their table, already completely drunk. Meghan didn't know much about Joanna, not having the opportunity to work many shifts with her, but she did know that Joanna was the only one in the team to be on a short-term contract. It was a fact Joanna harboured bitterness over, and happily complained about to everyone who would listen, and a good many more who wouldn't. Erica was Margaret's wing woman, a domineering brassy blonde, there was nothing particularly noticeable about her. A bland conversationalist with a sharp tongue and a spiteful streak, she had something nasty to say about everyone, including Margaret, and Meghan stayed as tight-lipped as possible in her presence.

Having come straight from work, Meghan felt rather underdressed. While guests around her sported formal suits, race day dresses and sparkly jewellery, Meghan wore black leggings under a City Chic fitted black tunic with capped sleeves, finished off with her favourite pair of shoes, ancient black ballet flats in desperate need of retiring. For a fleeting moment Meghan wished that she had taken the time to dress up, or at the very least had bothered to check her reflection. Single, Meghan had no one to impress, nor did she have any desire to have someone to impress, not really. At least, that is what she told herself. Despite the hum of the air conditioning, the room was stuffy, and Meghan excused herself from the table, squeezing her way through the barrage of patrons until she reached the back door, slipping out onto the covered patio and into the cool night air.

The patio was far less crowded than inside, with small groups of partygoers indulging in intimate conversations, and soft laughter floating around on the breeze. Meghan crossed to the rail and leaned on it, slipping her aching feet out of her shoes and breathing in deeply as she indulged in a spot of people watching.

"Oomph!" something hard and solid collided with Meghan, knocking her off balance, and her hands grasped the air, desperately looking for something to stop her from falling. "Careful," the rich timbre of the voice washed over Meghan as strong fingers bit into her elbow, steadying her. Balance restored, Meghan looked up, her startled gaze meeting the surprised gaze of someone all too familiar.

"Doctor James!" she snapped, breathless, as she tried to stop her pulse from racing. "What do you mean 'careful'? You ran into me!" she jabbed her index finger into his chest to illustrate her point. James threw back his head and laughed, the robust sound washing over those around him.

He was exhausted, having worked an unplanned double shift due to a drawn-out retrieval, but there was no way he was going to miss this work party. Although there were several work functions and parties held throughout the course of a year, this was the first one that he had been able to attend, and James put a high importance on maintaining old friendships and making new acquaintances. Once he had finally clocked off, he had returned to his basic staff accommodations, changed out of his navy-blue scrubs, donned his faithful denim jeans and a crisp linen shirt, and headed out to the Gillen Club. Spotting a group of his friends on the balcony he had made a beeline for them, accidentally running into Meghan in the process, literally. "I'm sorry," his eyes twinkled at her scowling expression. She certainly had spunk, a trait James found especially enticing. If he was looking, which he wasn't, he reminded himself firmly, before giving Meghan a cheeky wink and striding off to join his friends' table.

James surreptitiously watched as something caught Meghan's attention and she smiled, moving to join a table in the corner of the patio, greeted in true bear hug fashion by a male with adoration written all over his face. James thought that he had seen him floating around the emergency department but wasn't sure in what capacity. There was a familiarity to their embrace, and James wondered briefly if they were lovers, before shrugging and reminding himself that it was none of his business. Even so, James's eyes kept tracking back to Meghan's table, and he found it hard to concentrate on the conversation around him. He felt almost captivated by her, something that he had not felt for a very long time. In fact, it was well known that James was a workaholic, with zero tolerance for relationships. It was a status quo that he fiercely guarded and had no desire to change. James tore his gaze away from Meghan's table with difficulty and forced himself to ignore her for the rest of the night.

Meghan couldn't remember ever having enjoyed herself so much at a work function before and was starting to feel almost glad that she had come, when Alex broke off midsentence, grimaced over her shoulder, and warned in an undertone "Heads up Meghan, Stephen's on his way over and he looks especially determined." Great, the last thing Meghan wanted was yet another run-in with Stephen.

"Hey, I know you," the slurred voice blew hot air in Meghan's face as Stephen flopped himself down in the chair opposite her and slumped forward over the table.

"Yes Stephen, we both work at the hospital, remember?" Meghan sighed, giving him a once over. Seriously, there were scores of women at this party, most of whom would be happily looking for a date, why on Earth couldn't Stephen have chosen one of them to pin his affections on? Meghan had been rejecting Stephen for several weeks now, the man seemed completely unaffected by her refusals to date him, if anything, he seemed even more determined to pursue her. Despite the fact that Meghan did not date, not anymore, not since Michael, Stephen most certainly was not her type. She just had to find a way of making him re-alise it as well.

"How about we go somewhere less crowded?" Stephen waggled his eyebrows suggestively at Meghan, his gaze firmly planted on her chest.

"Stephen, I'm not interested," Meghan's voice sounded louder than she had intended, and she cringed, hoping no one had overheard her.

While she might not like Stephen, the last thing she wanted was for either of them to become hospital gossip. "AJ I think I'll head home, I'll call you later," Meghan stood and addressed Alex by his nickname, swinging her bag over her shoulder, and heading for the exit. Meghan smiled at the receptionist as she passed back through the foyer, stopping in the glow of the outside light to fish around in her handbag for her car keys.

"Hey, wait for a second," a hand snaked out and grabbed her wrist, jerking her backwards, snagging her ankle on the edge of the rocky garden bed. "I haven't finished talking to you yet."

James stepped through the front door and stopped, his eyes taking in the scene before him in a split second, the anxious, cautious look in Meghan's eyes, the way this man's fingers tightened on her wrist, the sneer on his face. James could already tell that her wrist would be bruised come tomorrow. "I don't mean to interrupt darling," James draped his arm around Meghan's shoulders, pulling her into a gentle embrace, forcing her wrist free as confusion and then understanding flashed in her eyes. "The babysitter called, Max has a fever, I told her we'd be right there." Nodding at the stranger, James led a limping Meghan away through the carpark, only stopping once they were in front of his charcoal black ute. James looked at Meghan and smiled. "I'm sorry about the little charade back there, but it seemed as if you could use a hand," his thick South African accent surrounding her like a warm hug.

"Thank you, I appreciate it," Meghan bent down to rub her ankle, wincing through the throbbing pain.

"May I?" James gestured towards her ankle. "You should probably have that checked just to make sure that nothing is broken." Meghan nodded, waiting while James unlocked the ute before ungraciously clamouring up into the front seat while he held the door out of her way.

Meghan stuck her foot in James's direction, trembling slightly as his fingers gently probed her ankle, concentration etched across his face.

"Good news," James glanced up, looking straight into Meghan's striking blue-grey eyes. "It's not broken, but it is sprained. I can strap it for you, which will help to minimise the swelling and bruising." Meghan nodded. "I'll just get my bag," James disappeared to the back of the ute, rummaging around before returning with a bandage and starting to strap her ankle, taking the opportunity to observe her properly. She was unexpectedly stunning, curvaceous with a heart-shaped face crowned with messy pixie hair in a shocking bubble gum pink. She seemed completely unaware of her charm, it was whimsical and enticing, and for James, very, very dangerous. "How is it that I have never run into you before, and then in the course of two days I see you everywhere? Are you new to town?"

"I was going to ask you the same thing," Meghan gasped as a sharp pain shot up her ankle. "I've been here for almost three years."

"I've been at the hospital for nearly five months, have you worked there this whole time?"

"Yes," Meghan answered hesitantly, avoiding James's gaze at all costs.

Odd, thought James. Everything about Meghan's last answer screamed that she would rather be anywhere else. She sounded almost vulnerable, her shoulders hunched in on herself as if she was wearing armour, her stormy blue-grey eyes had a look of deep sadness, of wariness. James already knew that Meghan was a nurse, she had told him so herself. Perhaps that was the problem, if Mr Mean at the front door was an issue for her, maybe she was worried that James would try to find her at work. "I work mostly out of the emergency department, I guess that's why our paths haven't crossed," James mused, trying to reassure Meghan.

"Most likely," Meghan began. "I work on the children's ward at the moment, although I trained in obstetrics."

"Why the switch?"

"Nothing sinister," Meghan hastened to explain. "I just had a personal crisis of sorts and needed some time to work out what I really wanted."

James was burning to know what this personal crisis was but sensed that even if he asked, Meghan would be less than willing to tell him. "There we go, all done," James fastened the bandage clip in place. "You won't be able to drive for a day or so, can I give you a lift home?"

"Thank you," Meghan smiled. "That would be lovely." The drive home was quiet, something Meghan was glad about. She hated making small talk and wasn't sure she would have been able to with James sitting in the car with her. His presence seemed to fill the car, surrounding her with his scent, a heady blend of imperial leather, sandalwood and antiseptic. It made Meghan feel comfortable and safe, something she could not afford to be. What a weird night this had turned out to be. With Alice Springs being as small as it was, it wasn't long before James was pulling his ute into the driveway of Meghan's house. Cutting the engine, he stepped out of the car and came around to Meghan's side, opening her door for her and offering a hand to help her step down. Meghan offered a smile of thanks, she was not used to riding in a ute and being rather uncoordinated, she was glad of the help before she fell and made a fool of herself.

James eyed Meghan's front steps with uncertainty before sneaking a sideways glance at her profile. "I don't like your chances of managing those steps. Let me carry you up, I will feel better once I know you are safely inside," James could literally see Meghan's hackles rise as he spoke, and waited, anticipating her refusal.

"Fine," Meghan sighed defeatedly, internally admitting that James was probably right, she would have struggled to manoeuvre up those steps, especially given her complete lack of coordination. James tried not to smile as he easily scooped her up into his arms. It wasn't that he was arrogant, or that he particularly enjoyed being right, it was more the way that she had sighed, all huffy, as if being carried – helpfully –

up the steps was a major hardship she had to bear. James chuckled to himself, it was kind of cute. Wait – what?! James's steps faltered as the surprising admission occurred to him. The last thing James needed, the very last thing, was to start thinking Meghan was cute. Get a grip man, commanded his stern inner voice. The last thing you need is to get tangled up in a relationship, or sex, or whatever else you were contemplating. James nodded, he was right. There was no way he was interested in a relationship, of any kind, at this point in his life. Not when things were finally back to normal.

Reaching the landing, James carefully placed Meghan on the stoop, holding her steady as she retrieved her house keys from her bag and unlocked the front door. Once opened, Meghan stepped through and turned to speak to James. "Thank you."

"My pleasure," James smiled. "Try to keep it elevated and iced. If you give me your car keys, I will drop your car back for you tomorrow."

Meghan took her keys and wriggled the car key off the keychain. "Thank you. Here," Meghan rummaged around in her bag and brought out a scrap of paper and ballpoint pen. "this is my number," she scribbled down a series of digits before passing it to James, "can you text me when you are on your way?"

"Sure," James glanced at the paper in his hand before tucking it into his pocket and smiling. "Go on, get that foot up, I'll see you tomorrow." He shooed her inside and gently started pulling the door closed.

"Good night James," Meghan said softly, before closing the door and turning the deadbolt with a loud clunk.

James started up his car and then sat, unmoving, deep in thought, until a car driving past backfired, startling him out of his reverie. Shifting into gear, he backed out slowly and headed home. Well, home for him at any rate. Not willing to commit to a long-term contract, James had opted for a standard six-month contract or the 'I'm not sure I can handle being away from civilisation for any longer' contract, as many of the hospital staff referred to it. He had been lucky enough to secure accommodation on-site at the hospital, a well maintained, albeit basic, one bedroomed apartment in their Waratah complex. James had been there for just short of five months now and was grateful every day that he had not opted for the cheaper Wattle accommodation, which he considered to be just a small step up from a tent! He visibly shuddered at the thought. James was not a camper. Letting himself into his apartment, James crossed to the small kitchen, pulling a glass from an overhead cabinet before rummaging in the fridge and producing a bottle of orange juice. Filling his glass, he downed it in a single pull, rinsing his glass and leaving it on the sink to drain, before crossing through the lounge room into the single bedroom.

Stripping his clothes off, he walked into the functional ensuite bathroom and turned the shower on, stepping into the warm water. As the water sluiced down his chiselled body, James felt his tense muscles start to relax, and the cobwebs from his head clear. He allowed himself to spend a guilty five minutes more in the shower than he usually would, shaking the water out of his eyes before stepping out of the shower and towelling off. Padding through to the bedroom, James switched both his mobile phone and his pager to silent and threw them into his bedside drawer. Not technically on call tonight, there was no need to be reachable, he knew the switchboard could always connect any trauma calls through to his apartment if the consultant on-call deemed the case serious enough to require James. Turning the knob on the ceiling fan to high, James slid between his cotton sheets, not bothering to stop and find pyjamas. His thoughts turned to Meghan, he wondered what her story was. As tempted as he was by her, he needed to remember to keep his distance, he had two more months left on his contract, and the last thing he needed was entanglements. Sleep eluded him, and he tossed and turned in an attempt to get his mind to switch off, before he finally succumbed, falling into a restless sleep just after midnight.

CHAPTER THREE

A loud knocking woke James and he headed for the door, hastily pulling on the jeans he had discarded the night before. He pulled the door open and smiled when he saw his friend standing there. "Xavier, you look beat." James stepped aside as Xavier entered, walking through to the kitchen.

"Two trauma cases last night, another one on the way in this morning," Xavier answered, helping himself to a mug and filling it with hot coffee from the pre-set percolator before sinking onto a stool at the breakfast bar.

"Do you need me to come in?" James sat on the stool opposite Xavier. Although it was his rostered day off, James knew that the hospital was perpetually understaffed, and a day off was never to be counted on as a sure thing.

"No, Jacobs will call you if things get any worse," Xavier stated, referring to their current Head of Surgery, Dr Jacobs. "So, how was the party last night? Tell me everything, who made a scene? Who was the funniest drunk? Who went home with who? Come on mate, give me all the juicy details."

"Seriously," James erupted with laughter, "You are worse than my Nanna Meg, and she died gossiping!"

"Okay, okay," Xavier raised his hands in surrender, "if you won't tell me I will just have to ask Amber."

"Amber? The blonde nurse from the emergency department? Are you still seeing her? Does this mean you are starting to get serious with someone other than yourself?" James chuckled at his own joke.

"Don't be ridiculous James, we both know I am not the marrying kind, just as we both know that I am not the celibate kind either." Xavier waggled his eyebrows up and down, causing James to groan.

"Seriously," James admonished, "you know I have to work with these people, I'm tired of hearing them cry in the tearoom after you break their hearts."

"Oh, come on!" Xavier huffed, "If their hearts are broken it is through no fault of mine, I am always upfront with them, they know where they stand before anything ever happens." At James's noncommittal sound, Xavier continues. "Besides, at least I am having fun while I am here, instead of locking myself away with work twenty-four hours a day. I mean, did you even speak to anyone at the party last night? Someone other than a direct colleague, someone like a female?"

"That's different," James protested.

"Why? Because Jessinta wounded your pride, or because she stole from you? Or maybe it is the fact that she broke your heart and you are pining for her? Seriously mate, it was months ago, move on, you can bet she already has." As much as James hated to admit it, he had a feeling that Xavier was probably right, about most things at least, although he was fairly sure that Jessinta had not, as everyone suspected, broken his heart. James wasn't even sure if he had really loved her, in his darkest moments he wondered if he was even capable of love, real, deep, unending love. Oh, he had enjoyed spending time with her, he had even entertained the possibility of cohabitating with her when she suggested it, and certainly hadn't refuted it when both sets of parents had started making plans for their future, but the simple fact was, it was her betrayal that smarted the most, not the end of the relationship.

"Alright, alright," James waved a hand in the air dismissively. "Although, actually, I did meet someone, sort of." Over the course of the next hour, and more coffee, James recounted the previous two days' encounters to Xavier, not feeling the need to edit anything out, trusting his friend implicitly.

"So, you're attracted to this girl?" Xavier stated, "And yet you still ended up spending the night alone," he shook his head sadly. James was impressed that Xavier had managed to wait until the end of the story to speak.

"Well," James conceded with a rueful smile, "we can't all be like you." James and Xavier, along with their mutual friend Matthew, had gone through the same university together and had been lucky enough to do their surgical residency at the same hospital. The three of them had formed an impenetrable bond through hard work and a mutual love of rock music and had become closer to each other than their own respective brothers.

James was the oldest, the responsible one who kept them, mostly, out of any serious trouble; Xavier Harvey was the likeable, well-known playboy, with no interest in settling down, completely content to simply enjoy the here and now without any commitment or consequence; and Matthew Goodwin, or Matt as he was known, was the youngest. He was also the hardest working of them all, with his father a prominent Head of Department at a prestigious inner Sydney hospital, he felt he needed to prove that he was a doctor on his own merits and not just on his father's influence, something that had never been in doubt as far as Xavier and James were concerned. While Matt and Xavier had remained in the surgical stream, James had qualified in both surgical and anaesthetics and was currently working with the Royal Flying Doctor Service as a retrieval doctor, a role he relished.

"That's the truth!" Xavier stood and drained his cup. "Okay, go, get this girl her car, call me later and tell me if anything happened, although knowing you, the answer will be a no," he gave James a friendly slap on his back.

"Fine," James smiled and saw his friend to the door. "I'll call you later, maybe we could all do dinner tomorrow if we can manage to finish on time. I'll call Matt this afternoon and see if he will be free." After seeing Xavier out, James took a quick shower and dressed, pausing to take a moment to program Meghan's phone number into his mobile, before donning his worn sneakers. Collecting his wallet and Meghan's car key off the bench, he headed into town. The walk from the hospital to the venue of last's night's work function was only a short distance, and James easily covered it within fifteen minutes. Sliding into the driver's seat, James pulled his mobile out and sent a quick text message to Meghan, letting her know that he was about to head over. Her reply was immediate, she was at home and would see him shortly. Shifting into gear, James again drove the short distance to Meghan's house, pulling into her driveway minutes later. Making sure to adjust the seat back to the original position, James jogged up the few steps leading to her front door and knocked.

Meghan pulled the door open and blinked, her gaze meeting James's hard chest before slowly gliding upwards to meet his amused gaze. "Hi," she swallowed thickly, all too aware of just how very male James was. "Thanks for doing this, I appreciate it." She cleared her throat awkwardly, her hand gesturing vaguely in the direction of her car as she struggled to keep her eyes from wandering back down over James's muscled body.

"It was my pleasure," a slow smile unfurled across James's face. "How is your ankle feeling this morning?"

"A bit sore, but I'll manage," Meghan smiled ruefully up at him. "Let me guess, you want to check it out just to be sure?"

A raucous laugh erupted unexpectedly from James. "You make it sound like it is something to be endured! Come on, it won't take long," and with that, James pushed past Meghan into her house.

James wasn't quite sure what he was expecting, but it certainly wasn't this. From the outside, Meghan's house was nondescript, like the majority of the properties in and around Alice Springs, the outside consisted mainly of red dirt and nasty three-cornered prickles, devoid of any real effort or personalisation. It just wasn't worth the effort in Alice Springs, the desert climate made it virtually impossible for anything resembling grass or a garden to grow successfully unless you had copious amounts of money and an endless supply of time to spend on it. A drive around the town is testament to that, with streets full of concrete block houses and iron sheeting fences, if any. It was only when one drove over to the golf course side of town, known to be where the Americans from the local Pine Gap spy base lived, that you started to see lush green grass and actual gardens. James had been a guest in several of the homes in that area, and they were just as rich and luscious on the inside as they appeared on the outside. The inside of Meghan's house, however, was an oasis against the scorching heat outside. The spacious lounge room was furnished with a mismatched assortment of brightly coloured armchairs, soft cotton lounges, and a violent green velvet recliner. A large coffee table sat in the middle of a fuchsia rug, flanked by two oddly sculpted lamps, and holding a round tub of flowering cacti. Every single inch of available wall was taken up with bookcases, although that was clearly not enough, as there were also stacks of books piled in front of the bookcases.

"So, a reader then," James joked, grinning at Meghan, who merely rolled her eyes at him and brushed past, hobbling over to the couch and sinking down into it with a pointed look at her ankle. James crossed to join her, moving the tub of cacti before perching on the edge of the coffee table and drawing her ankle up to his lap, while Meghan watched with a look of bemusement on her face. James winked and dipped his head, concentration etched across his face as he carefully started to feel his way down her foot towards her ankle. Meghan swallowed the lump in her throat and clenched her jaw tightly shut, refusing to allow it to gape open as it wanted to at the sight of James hunched over her ankle, his khaki coloured tee pulled tightly across his chest, his biceps bulging. Good lord, he was gorgeous! Meghan let her eyes travel across his chest, wondering if it felt as hard as it looked. Enough! Meghan scolded herself, don't you dare look at him that way, there is no way he is your type, he's just another Michael, do you want to end up hurt again? Meghan sighed regretfully, she hated it when her inner voice was right, which was usually always.

A stab of pain drew Meghan's eyes away from James's chest and to her ankle, currently being probed by James's slender fingers. "Sorry," winced James. Meghan knew she should move her eyes, look away, look anywhere but at her ankle resting in James's lap. She could see his taut thighs straining against the fabric of his jeans, her mouth going dry at the thought of what lay beneath. Aching, itching to reach out and touch him, Meghan curled her treacherous fingers into a ball and squashed them in between her knees. A cough from James jerked Meghan out of her reverie and brought her back to her senses. She looked up, directly into James's amused eyes. "See anything you like?" he teased. Seeing the way Meghan blushed a deep shade of crimson, James decided that she had definitely found something she liked, which was a very interesting thought indeed. "All done," James released her ankle,

placing her foot gently on the ground, then, without overthinking it, leant forward, cupped her face in his hands, and kissed her.

Meghan gasped with surprise as James's lips pressed against hers, lips parting involuntarily, heat pooling in between her thighs, dampening the scrap of silk she wore underneath her dress. Meghan had never before experienced such a powerful reaction to a kiss, and she linked her hands together behind his head, urging him closer. James's tongue nudged her lips, seeking, and being granted, access. His tongue was silk, Meghan decided, as it danced with hers, duelling for dominance, probing her mouth, tasting and sucking. His hands moved to her back, drawing her closer to his chest, angling her head in order to deepen the kiss. Sliding her fingers over his bald scalp she pressed his mouth closer still, arching her back against him and groaning into the kiss, feeling him smile as she did so. The kiss ended all too soon, leaving Meghan momentarily disorientated. "That was-"

"A mistake," Meghan gasped out hastily, cutting James off midsentence.

"Really?" James cocked an eyebrow, surprise lacing his words. "You think so?".

"Of course," Meghan stated emphatically, fighting to steady her breathing, "Don't you? I mean, we don't even know each other, you work at the same small hospital as I do, obviously, this is Alice Springs," Meghan was aware she was babbling but unable to stop herself, "and even if that wasn't the case, I am not looking for a relationship. Of any kind," she finished in a rush.

"I think that was fun," James countered, "and I would like to..." he trailed off, dipping his head to feather kisses along Meghan's jawline and down her slender neck.

"Enough!" Meghan's voice squeaked, and she shoved James away with a firmness she wasn't feeling.

"If you want me to go, Meghan, I will," James stated simply, standing up. A hungry look clouded his eyes as his gaze raked over Meghan. "Your body betrays you," he gestures to Meghan's breasts, her hardened nipples visible beneath her shirt. "You want me as much as I want you," and with that, he strode out, leaving Meghan gaping open-mouthed after him.

CHAPTER FOUR

"What a pig!" Meghan spat out, slamming the phone down in disgust. She pulled the communal work diary off the shelf and turned to today's page, writing without stopping, until satisfied, she shut the diary and passed it over to her co-worker to read.

"Blake?" Tessa shook her head incredulously. It was a currently accepted fact that Blake Stanley, orthopaedic surgeon, was a complete arse to everyone he met, more so to the nursing staff, who he seemed to think were there to act as his very own personal assistants and couldn't fathom why they refused to do the simple tasks that he requested, like collect his mail and sort out his shopping. She wondered if Blake would ever fit in here, in Alice Springs things were so vastly different from anywhere else in Australia, the world really, and not at all what he was used to in his usual role as an orthopaedic surgeon at the prestigious Melbourne Alfred Hospital.

Tessa had been attached to the children's ward for nearly as long as Meghan. In her mid-thirties, she was a devout Christian who was honest to a fault. The majority of her shifts coincided with Meghan's, and the two women had become firm friends during the two years they had worked together, happy to discover that they had quite a few things in common outside of work as well. Meghan had been out of sorts all day, and she knew exactly what, or rather who, was to blame. Meghan had been so frustrated after James had left yesterday that she had been unable to concentrate on anything other than the way his mouth had felt on hers. Determined to block it out, she had treated herself to a homemade orange cake. Or rather, she would have treated herself to a homemade orange cake had she remembered that it was in the oven, instead of sitting in her recliner staring into space, daydreaming about kissing James again. Sighing deeply, Meghan got up and walked through to the adjoining kitchenette to make both herself and Tessa a strong cup of coffee. She had rung Tessa after the whole orange cake debacle, and Tessa had listened intently to Meghan as she related the day's events to her, before offering her rather surprising advice.

"Just sleep with him and get it out of your system," Tessa had stated simply, shocking Meghan. "Seriously, who cares? You are both adults, no one is married, have some fun while you can." It was the last thing that Meghan had expected to hear from Tessa, and she replayed the conversation in her head as she made the coffee, Tessa's advice swirling around inside her head, intermingling with the vision of Meghan kissing James. By the time the kettle had boiled, Meghan was more confused than ever. She was attracted to James, of that there was no mistake, she just wasn't sure that she would be able to have fun with James while Michael was still haunting her memories. She knew that she could come across as standoffish at times, she just didn't do casual very well. Ever, in fact. Not that she hadn't been tempted, she certainly had been, it was just that Meghan was a woman who liked to know exactly what was happening and exactly when, an insecurity leftover from her childhood in and out of foster homes. Was Meghan wrong to feel the way that she did? It was a thought that plagued her for the rest of her shift and still remained unanswered as she drove out of the hospital carpark and headed for home late that afternoon.

James looked out of the window as the small plane taxied along the makeshift runway and up into the clear blue sky of the outback. The call had come in during the night, a pregnant woman had gone into spontaneous labour at thirty-six weeks, and with the nearest clinic currently unstaffed, James had been tasked with the job of retrieving the patient and transporting her, and her anxious husband, to the Alice Springs hospital. James's job had taken an unexpected turn however, once he had arrived at the outback station, he had found the young mother to be well and truly in active labour. Deciding that there was no time to return to the Alice Springs hospital, and knowing it would be more comfortable for the mother to give birth if they weren't battling turbulence, he had made the decision to stay grounded until the baby arrived. Settling the mother to be into the back of the Royal Flying Doctor Service aircraft, husband by her side, they prepared themselves for a wait. Less than half an hour later the lusty cry of Lucas John Gibson was heard from inside the aircraft, and James dispatched the new father to inform the extended family waiting outside, while he attended to the mother and her baby. Both appeared to be in a healthy condition, despite the early arrival, and after a tearful cuddle, James removed Lucas from his mother and placed him in the Neonatal Intensive Care Unit humidi-crib for transport back to Alice Springs.

Landing in Alice Springs, they were met by an ambulance that took them the short twenty-minute journey to the hospital. James accompanied them through to the Neonatal Intensive Care Unit, where Lucas would be thoroughly assessed by a paediatrician before being allowed to re-join his mother in the Maternity Unit. After handing over his patients, James headed for the dedicated retrieval office to complete his call out paperwork before shift change, hoping to be able to leave on time tonight if, at all possible, he was looking forward to a night of pizza, beer and cards with Xavier and Matt. Finishing his paperwork, he clocked off, only fifteen minutes late instead of the usual forty, and made a mental note to adjust his timesheet tomorrow. He took the long way to his accommodation, more for the exercise than the fact that it would take him directly past the children's ward, he reasoned with himself. James slowed his steps as he passed by the children's ward, debating whether or not to stop and talk to Meghan, before deciding against it. He had no way of knowing if she was even at work today, or what shift she would be on, and he doubted very much that she would appreciate him asking her colleagues. Besides, she had made her choice quite clear last week, and he respected that. Still, he couldn't help but glance inside the children's ward nurses' station as he walked past, surprised at the feeling of disappointment in the pit of his stomach when he saw that it wasn't in fact Meghan who was currently working.

His mood brightened when he saw Xavier and Matt loitering outside the lifts, deep in conversation, oblivious to all around them. "Seriously," he greeted them with a grin, "don't you have anything better to do than stand around gossiping?"

"Ha! Just waiting for you, nice detour by the way," Xavier replied casually, smirking, leaving James in no doubt as to what the topic of conversation would be tonight. Laughing, they headed off towards the staff accommodation, coming to an abrupt halt outside the hospital kitchen, Meghan rushing through the automatic kitchen doors and colliding face first with James's chest.

"See, I knew you couldn't resist me," James joked straight-faced, straightening her up and looking pointedly at the blue hair cap adorning her head. "Nice hat."

"Thanks," Meghan scrunched up her nose, reaching up to pull off the hair net before wadding it up and shoving it in her pocket. "Matt," Meghan beamed, noticing the men standing with James. "I didn't know you were back, how's your dad?" James seethed with resentment, why was Meghan so happy to see Matt, but not him? She hadn't greeted him with her beaming smile, was it possible that she wasn't interested in James because she fancied Matt instead? Surgeons did tend to be the rock stars of the medical world.

"He's really good," Matt answered. "He is actually off to France next week to speak at a conference on trauma management in rural settings. Mum is thrilled," Matt confided conspiratorially, "Dad has promised her a two-week holiday before they return to Australia. How about you? Starting or finishing your shift?"

"Finishing, thank god!" Meghan shuddered. "This day has been a madhouse."

"Oh no, Blake again?" Matt sympathised. "I heard you had a run-in with him last week, it has become quite the staffroom story. Did you really tell him to send his laundry home to his mother if he couldn't man up and learn to use the washing machines here?" Matt finished on a chuckle, just imagining Meghan saying that.

"Something like that," Meghan blushed, stealing a glance at James. She wondered if he had also heard the story, and what his opinion was, but she was met with a stony glare from James. "Well, I better go, have a nice night," she finished meekly, frowning in confusion at James before heading off in the direction of the children's ward, leaving them looking after her.

"You're an idiot," Xavier addressed James, playfully punching him on the shoulder. "You should have asked her out. You heard her, she has had a bad day, you could have taken her out and cheered her up."

"Maybe Matt should be the one asking her out," James bit out sarcastically, before turning on his heel and stomping off.

"James, wait up," Matt called after him, ducking around an oncoming gurney. James slowed his steps, stopping in a shaded courtyard to wait for his friends to catch up, not missing the pointed look that passed between them. "James, Meghan and I have both worked the midnight shift on and off for weeks now, you know I would never-"

"I know," James sighed deeply. "I'm sorry, I was being a prat."

"You were being jealous," Xavier rubbed his hands together in glee, eyes shining.

"Fine. I was being jealous," James snapped.

"I knew it!" Triumphed Xavier. "You know what you should do?" he asked, earning groans from both matt and James. "Now, now, hear me out."

"As long as it's legal," quipped James.

"And doesn't cause a riot," added Matt.

"Seriously, that was *one* time," defended Xavier. "What you need to do James, is march right over there and kiss her. Simple."

"Trouble is, Xavier, I already tried that, last week, when I took her car back."

"You what?!" Xavier was speechless. "Why didn't you tell us? This is huge!"

"There is a long list of reasons as to why you weren't the first person I called Xavier, the first being that we aren't in third grade," James jested. "Besides, she threw me out," James finished sheepishly.

"Now this is a story I need to hear," Matt smiled. "Come on, there's beer at my place, and the pizza should be there soon."

When Meghan arrived home from work the following day it was to find James sitting on her front stoop, waiting for her with a smile capable of melting even the strongest of defences.

"James, the ankle is fine," Meghan spoke as she walked toward him.

"I'm glad to hear that, but I'm here about the other issue," James smiled, scooting out of the way as she unlocked the door and let them both in.

"What other issue?" Meghan led the way through to the kitchen where she dumped her bag before putting the kettle on to boil. "Coffee?"

"No thank you, I want you," James said simply. Meghan placed her coffee cup on the bench and turned slowly to face James, mouth agape, staring at him for a moment before speaking.

"Get out," she ordered.

"Just hear me out," James held his hands up in surrender, "two minutes is all I need, please."

"Fine, two minutes," Meghan conceded, crossing her arms over her chest and glaring at James.

"I don't want a relationship," James started. "I mean, I am not looking for a serious relationship," he amended, sighing. "Let me start that again. I am attracted to you," he smiled wickedly at Meghan. "I don't know why, but there is something about you that intrigues me. I don't care that we don't know each other, or that we work together. I am the definition of discreet. I'm not looking for a commitment, Meghan, I just want to spend time with you and see what happens," James watched

Meghan as he spoke, he wondered if she knew how expressive her face was? He knew she was afraid, of what he didn't know, but he had to reassure her, to make her see that she had nothing to fear from him "I won't hurt you, Meg, you have my word". It felt right for James to shorten her name, and he saw the corner of her mouth lift in a smile as he did.

"You're right," she said softly, her mind made up. "You won't hurt me, now get out," she stood firm, arms crossed over her chest, refusing to budge.

He may be as sexy as hell, he may have a smile that could turn her to mush, but there was no way she was going to act on it. She had already learnt her lesson as far men were concerned and she was in no hurry to repeat her past mistakes, no matter how incredibly tempting he was. Even though she had thrown him out, even though she knew it had to be this way, that it was for the best, Meghan couldn't help but feel empty as she shut the door after him. He hadn't even argued, and the fact that she felt annoyed by this niggled at her subconscious, long after James's car had gone from view.

CHAPTER FIVE

If Meghan had been confused before, it was nothing in comparison to how she was feeling now. Barely able to sleep the night before, she had dragged herself through the shower and dug out her stash of barely used makeup in an attempt to make herself presentable. Finding somewhere to park at the Alice Springs hospital was a nightmare, and by the time Meghan had found a free space to pull into, she was running late for work. Meghan hurried across the parking lot and through the front doors, walking with sure steps. She loved her job, loved the constant hustle of it all. She knew some people thought of nursing staff as no more than receptionists, standing around waiting to snare a doctor before retiring to have chubby babies, but she knew better. Meghan fished her staff keys and ID card out of her bag, promptly dropping them on the floor as she caught sight of James at the other end of the corridor. Blushing a deep crimson, Meghan fumbled to pick them up, finally getting the children's ward door open and slipping inside. She pushed the door closed and leaned on the back of it with a relieved sigh, praying that no one would notice just how breathless she was.

The day was frantic, and Meghan was grateful to be busy. Around midmorning Meghan spotted smoke curling from underneath the door of a patient's room, activating the fire alarm and ripping the fire extinguisher off the wall in the corridor, before shouldering the door open, stunned at the sight that greeted her. Felix was sitting in the middle of his bed, surrounded by fire, a box of matches in his hands. It hadn't taken long to extinguish the flames, and Felix had been treated for serious burns, before being transferred to the ward next door, a specialist psychiatric ward. The ward nurse in charge had made Meghan a strong cup of sweet tea, ushering her into the staff-only garden with strict orders not to return until she was ready. Sitting in the shaded courtyard, Meghan was unaware that someone had joined her, jumping in shock when James spoke to her.

"You need to drink this," the now cool tea was pressed into her still shaking hands. Keeping his hands there, James guided the cup to her lips, only removing them when he was satisfied that Meghan was drinking. They sat in silence, legs touching, until Meghan drained her cup and stood, placing a hand on his cheek.

"Thank you," she whispered, turning and heading back to work.

By the time her shift ended Meghan was exhausted and very relieved to be logging out. She walked out with Tessa, going the long way around, through the maze of staff-only corridors and coming out at the staff carpark. Hugging goodbye, Meghan walked to her car and hopped in, throwing her bag and lunch box on the passenger seat. Meghan wound down the front windows and turned the key in the ignition, forcing the old engine to splutter to life. She waved as Tessa drove past and beeped her horn, then put on her seat belt and shifted into reverse, checking her rear-view mirror and nearing suffering a heart attack in the process. James, larger than life, was standing behind the car, grinning like the proverbial Cheshire cat, making Meghan instantly suspicious. Slamming both feet on the brake and stalling the car, Meghan yanked open the door and stormed out, rounding on James with a fiery look in her eyes. "Are you insane?" she didn't care that she was yelling, or who might hear her. "Do you have a death wish? I could have killed you!"

"I trusted that you would be a cautious driver," James shrugged, completely unfazed. He liked this side of Meghan, this independent, fierce side.

"Humph, you nearly gave me heart failure," she shook her head. "Honestly!"

"Don't worry Meghan," James stepped close enough to whisper in her ear, "I know CPR." The seductive way in which he whispered sent shivers down her spine, and her lips parted slightly, yearning to kiss him. He looked at her, eyes round, face flushed, and smiled slowly. "Have coffee with me?" Meghan studied his face and thought his request over. She was tired of always going home alone, what would it hurt, to have coffee with a friend?

"As friends?" She clarified.

"If that is what you would like us to be," James confirmed.

"Then yes, I would love to have coffee with you, James," she watched as his face stretched into a grin. "How about my place? In twenty minutes, if you are already finished for the day?"

"I'll be there," James kissed her cheek and held her car door open for her. "Drive carefully Meghan, watch out for crazy pedestrians". He waved her off and then headed back to his unit to change, humming all the way.

Once home Meghan raced around tidying up and then headed into the bathroom to change. As she raced through shaving her legs and shampooing her hair, moisturised and plucked, primped and preened, she reminded herself that this was *not* a big deal, that this was in fact only coffee with a friend. A sexy, virile friend, who she had no designs on. Yeah, right, her reflection in the mirror taunted her, you are such a liar. In any case, she told herself firmly, there was no harm in looking nice. When James knocked on the door, right on time, he was stunned by the sight that greeted him. Meghan looked stunning, fresh-faced and down to earth. Wearing a sea-green summer dress that swished around her knees as she walked, and looked as soft as silk, James couldn't take his eyes off her, feeling rather smug with himself when she blushed under his appreciative gaze. Desire flared inside him as he watched her move around, and he hastened to sit at the table before he embarrassed himself, the jeans he wore were way too tight for hiding his arousal.

Meghan kept up a steady stream of conversation as they enjoyed their coffee, she was fascinated by James's work and what drove him, and completely mesmerised by his thick South African accent and the way it flowed around the room. He surprised her by having a wicked sense of humour and happily regaled her with stories of mischief from his university days with Matthew and Xavier, which had her in peals of laughter. It was nice to discover this other side of James, away from the formality of the Alice Springs hospital and the revered role he played in shaping and managing the way in which a retrieval rescue was carried out. His whole persona relaxed, he was more grounded and approachable. Meghan was grateful to be seeing this other side of James, she got the impression that it was a side he didn't let a lot of people witness. She was infinity more attracted to him, seeing his relaxed side, and was shocked when she glanced at the clock and saw that nearly two hours had passed since they first sat down.

As James rose to go Meghan realised she felt restless, unsettled. "James," she stopped him with a hand on his arm, the muscles rippling beneath her touch. "You told me yesterday that you wouldn't hurt me, I want to know, how can you be so sure of that?" Meghan held her breath, waiting.

"I don't know what happened to make you so afraid Meghan, but I give you my word, as long as it is in my power, I will never intentionally hurt you." He spoke with such certainty in his voice, such a conviction in his words, that Meghan didn't doubt him.

"I am not looking for a relationship James, and that will never change," she spoke cautiously, wanting to ensure that he really understood her, that he knew this was non-negotiable for her. "You were right, though," she conceded. "I am attracted to you."

"Say that again," James smirked.

"You were right," Meghan repeated.

"No, the other part," James prompted.

"I am attracted to you," Meghan smiled.

"You're attracted to me," James grinned, "and I am attracted to you," he brought his lips down to meet Meghan's, slowly, gently, relishing in the feel of her mouth on his, breaking away reluctantly. "I should go."

"Or you could stay," Meghan gathered the front of his shirt in her hands.

"Meghan," James groaned, his resolve slipping. "If I stay..." he moved away from her, his sentence hung in the air between them.

"No strings attached, James," Meghan began, "that's what you said. I trust you to keep your word, and there is no possibility of me ever wanting more from you than that. So, stay," she shrugged, "I want you to stay, I want you," she finished forcefully, the confidence of knowing what she wanted from James showing through in her self-assured voice.

"I want you too," James crossed to Meghan in a single stride, cupping her face gently in both of his hands and bringing his mouth down to hers, his tongue softly parting her lips, entering her mouth with confidence. His fingers tangled in her hair and he angled her face, his tongue delving deeper inside, tasting every inch he could. She tasted like peppermint, it tingled against his tongue and reminded him of Christmas mornings.

"Meghan are you sure?" James tore himself away from her mouth to ask. He had to know this was what she wanted too, not just because she was caught up in the moment, he had to hear her say it. Meghan thought about what James had said for approximately three seconds before standing up and pulling his mouth back down to hers. "I'm sure," she stated, knowing that he needed to hear her say it. Tessa was right, she should have some fun while she could. Meghan had been a prisoner of her past for too long, keeping herself closed off from everyone lest they discover her secret. James felt different. Maybe it was the fact that he was only in Alice Springs for a short while, or maybe it was the deep sense of calm she felt whenever he was around. Whatever the reason, Meghan wanted him, and if the bulge in his pants was anything to go by, he wanted her just as much. They were both consenting adults, why shouldn't they throw caution to the wind and have some fun.

"Meghan!" James gasped, as her hands dipped inside his jeans and slid under the waistband of his boxer shorts, taking a firm grip on his shaft and starting to slide her hand up and down.

"What?" she asked innocently, before silencing any further complaints by taking his mouth in her own until he could no longer think coherently, let alone speak. "James," she slid her free hand down the front of his shirt, stopping at the waistband of his jeans, "don't think, just feel," Meghan slid her hand stroking James's shaft back up to his waistband, unfastening the fly and swiftly pulling down both his jeans and his boxer shorts, dropping to her knees as she did, before James could register what she was intending to do. "Gorgeous", breathed Meghan, taking in the sight of James's naked body, just as chiselled as she had imagined it would be.

Kneeling before him, smiling up at him with such unrestrained appreciation on her face, James thought he had never seen anything so beautiful. "Meg, you don't have to," he ground out, every word an effort to speak.

"Shh, I want to." Eyes never leaving his face, Meghan trailed her fingers up his inner thighs, softly caressing, before taking a delicate testicle into her mouth, causing James to cry out in surprise. Meghan sucked gently, rolling his aching testicle around her tongue, releasing it with a soft nip, before repeating the same ministrations to the other testicle. Rock hard, and standing erect, James wasn't sure how much longer he would last, his hand moving down with the intention of releasing his need. Slapping his hand away, still not breaking eye contact, Meghan shifted her mouth to his aching shaft, her tongue darting around the rim and over the top, fingers tickling the underside. She slid her hands up and around, grabbing onto his buttocks as she slid her waiting mouth over his hardened length, drawing him deep inside.

James buried his hands in Meghan's hair, watching her head bob back and forth, her wide eyes twinkling up at him. Watching his length slide in and out of her tight mouth, James had never seen anything so hot and was sure he would explode. Meghan's teeth grazed along his length as she slid her mouth up and down his shaft, painstakingly slowly, before building up a rhythm, faster and faster, before slowing back down, determined to draw out his pleasure for as long as she could.

"Meghan, I won't last much longer, I'm going to come!" James ground out, his voice impatient with need. "I can't...hold on...much longer!" Meghan tightened her hold on his buttocks and took his shaft even deeper into her mouth, humming as she did, sending vibrations shooting down his length. "Meghan!" James cried out triumphantly and clung to her hair as his orgasm tore through his body. He was vaguely aware of Meghan holding him in place until he went limp inside her, of her licking him clean before kissing his swollen head, but beyond that, he was incapable of coherent thought.

Regaining his composure, James pulled Meghan up into his arms, his mouth meeting hers. He could taste himself in her mouth and grew hard again at the thought. He broke contact in order to strip off his shirt, then scooped her into his arms, kicking his jeans and boxer shorts off of his ankles, leaving them where they lay on the kitchen floor. "Bedroom?" Meghan pointed to the end of the hall and James carried her through, placing her at the end of her large king-sized bed, stripping her of her dress and removing her bra and panties, leaving her standing completely naked in front of him.

"Breathtaking," James took her all in, his eyes hungrily eating her up. His hand reached out and traced her nipple, causing it to pucker at his touch. He wrapped his arms around Meghan, drawing her close, his mouth bending down to enclose her puckered nipple, earning a deeply satisfied moan from Meghan. He flicked his tongue over it, suckling it before nipping it between his teeth, causing Meghan to cry out and arch her back, thrusting her breasts towards him.

He moved to suckle her other breast, letting his hand trail down to her wet core between them, slipping two fingers inside her silky folds, feeling her pool of wetness wrap around him. He brought his fingers up to his mouth, tasting her, delighting in the way her eyes rounded as she watched him. He moved his fingers back to her core, tweaking her sensitive nub, feeling her writhe against him, trying to get closer, whimpering with need. Knowing she was ready for him, James pounded his fingers in and out of her dripping core, twisting them with each thrust, increasing his rhythm faster and faster, relishing the feel of her moving in sync against his fingers, thrusting her hips to take his fingers deeper inside her centre, moaning and screaming out his name as she came undone, shudders echoing through her body. Knowing that he had been responsible for her pleasure made his need even more urgent, and he turned her around to face the bed, guiding her into the middle and bending her over, his hard length shuddering in anticipation as she went down willingly, sighing his name as she did.

With her legs parted and her buttocks in the air, James could see just how wet Meghan already was for him, and with a low groan, he bent his head to taste her,

to suckle on her sensitive nub, slowly kissing her delicate folds as she mewed in delight, encouraging him. Needing no further urging, James plunged his tongue deep inside her core and ran it back and forth along the inside length of her, drinking in her wetness, savouring her taste. He moaned into her, flicked his tongue over her nub and then drew back, straightening up. He gripped his throbbing length in his hand, using it as a guide to thrust his thick shaft deep into her softness from behind, a deep sigh of satisfaction leaving his body as her walls stretched to accommodate his length with a delighted shout from Meghan.

James bent his body over Meghan's back, sliding an arm over the curve of her spine and around to her front, using his fingers to touch and tease her bundle of nerves as he moved inside her. Meghan urged him on with excited grunts and pleading, her hips thrusting as he moved in and out of her from behind, with exquisite slowness. He revelled in playing with her slick wetness with his fingers, relishing the very feel of her, rocking back and forth into her with long, slow, firm, deep strokes until he felt her climax building again. James began to move faster, frantic with need, so close to his release, rocking Meghan in rhythm, fuelled by her cries for him to go faster, harder, deeper. Exploding together, Meghan's walls gripped James's shaft tightly as he emptied his need deep inside of her, filling her. As they collapsed on top of the bed, limbs entwined, totally spent, James was struck with the thought that being with Meghan had felt absolutely perfect, and for the first time in his life, he had forgotten to use any precautions.

CHAPTER SIX

Meghan woke to the feel of James trailing his fingers up and down her spine, and sunlight pouring through her curtains. She rolled over groggily and stretched, smiling up at James from between her lashes, the memory of last night lingering in the air between them. She ached in places she didn't even know existed. They had spent the entire night discovering each other, demonstrating just how attracted they were to each other, falling asleep as the sun started to turn the sky a vibrant shade of blush pink. James's gaze raked over her body, a slow flush tinted her cheeks and she self-consciously reached for the sheet, discarded sometime during the night. A deep laugh rumbled up from James. "Leave it, you're exquisite," he instructed, drawing Meghan closer and claiming her mouth with a kiss that left her in no doubt as to his desire for her. He slid a hand down to her centre, growing hard when he discovered that she was already wet for him. Shifting position, he pushed her knees up, letting them fall to her sides. She was completely open for him, splayed out, leaving nothing hidden. He grinned wickedly up at her before teasing her sensitive nub with his tongue, claiming it with his mouth and sucking gently, as she writhed beneath him. He moved down to her silky folds, sliding his tongue inside, teasing, tasting her juices. Pulling her knees over his shoulders, he continued to slide his tongue in and out, flicking her nub with his fingers, pinching, rolling it between his thumb and forefinger as she bucked her hips beneath him, her breathing growing shallow.

"James!" she pleaded, clutching at his hips, "please!"

"Please what? Tell me what you need honey." His breath sent a cool breeze over her core, increasing her sensitivity. He wanted to hear her say it, he needed to hear it.

"I want you. Inside me. Now!" she panted. James smiled, reaching over to the bedside table he extracted a condom from his wallet, and unwrapped it, slipping it on. After their first-time last night, he had been certain to use protection, he had promised Meghan he wouldn't hurt her and as far as he was concerned, that also meant protecting her against any unwanted consequences. After his equilibrium had returned last night, he had confessed to Meghan that he had been too caught up in the moment to furnish protection and had been beyond relieved when she had smiled and told him that she was on the contraceptive pill. With Meghan's legs still dangling over his shoulders, he rose to his knees, leaning over her and using her legs as support, he drove his hardened length into her, before pulling out fully and driving in again and again. Meghan arched her back and bucked her hips to meet his powerful thrusts, screaming in pleasure as he drove in harder and deeper, his thick member hitting her G spot. "James, oh my god, James, yes, yes!" Meghan held nothing back as he moved within her, caressing his ego with her mews and moans, urging him deeper with her words.

"Come for me Meg," James ordered, knowing she was close. Pulling his length out fully, he gave one final thrust all the way into her core and felt her walls tighten around his stiffened member as he pushed her over the edge, hearing her scream out his name with wild abandon. With one final thrust he exploded inside her, gripping her hips for support until totally spent, he collapsed beside her.

The rest of the morning passed in a blur of lovemaking and discovery, with neither James nor Meghan in any hurry to move. It was with obvious reluctance that they eventually moved from the bed, James to catch up with his friends for dinner, and Meghan to get ready for her shift at the hospital. Meghan watched him unabashedly from her perch on the bed, as he showered and then dressed, scooting across to wrap her naked body around him as he sat on the edge of the bed to put his shoes on. He pulled her around so that she was sitting on his lap, and kissed her deeply, allowing his hands to roam freely over her curves, breaking away suddenly with an apologetic look in his eyes. "Sorry Meg, but if we keep that up, I will need another shower."

"Go," she laughingly replied, gently pushing him away, "enjoy your dinner, I will see you when I see you." As it happened, he called her from his Waratah unit as soon as he was back home from dinner, not trusting himself to walk down to the children's ward and talk with her face to face, just in case another staff member walked by and overheard them. As long as they were both working in the same remote hospital, he would be as discreet as it was possible to be.

The next few days passed in a happy blur for Meghan as a routine of sorts was established between her and James. While Meghan was rostered on the late shift, James would meet her at her house after her finishing time of midnight, kissing her with such desire it left her light-headed. Sometimes they would share a meal, more often than not they would forgo food, opting to luxuriate in each other's touches and caresses instead. Unless he was on an early shift the following day, James stayed the night, delighting in showing her just how much he had missed her. He seemed intent on mapping and memorising every inch of her body, with both his hands and his lips. He delighted in discovering what made her moan, what drew a contented purr from her lips, and what had her screaming his name the loudest. The fact that she was comfortable in her own skin, that she didn't censure or turn down her responses to him, was something James found incredibly sexy and he wondered if he would ever tire of being with her, of having her wrapped around him.

As the week neared the end, Meghan found herself back on day shifts, while James's shifts changed to nights. It was to be expected, both working shift work for a hospital, but it still felt odd to be in her house without James. Deciding to view it as a test for when James eventually moved on, Meghan filled her nights with spring cleaning and baking, much to the delight of the other ward nurses, who happily tucked into the various dishes Meghan furnished them with. Not wanting to eat everything herself, Meghan would bring boxes and containers of baked goods in to work each day, and the nursing staff would snack whenever they got a free moment. Which is how James found them, mid-afternoon, enjoying Meghan's double fudge triple chocolate chip brownies, as he walked past the nurses' station mid-shift. Stopping a short distance away, he pulled out his mobile and rang the extension for the nurses' station, smiling as he heard Meghan's chirpy business-like answer. "You look delectable in that dress," he teased, hearing her delighted gasp of recognition. "This is my last night shift, I have the next three days off, how about you?"

"I finish at six tonight, and then I am not back at work until next Wednesday. Will I see you for breakfast?"

"I can't wait," he spoke into the phone, teasing her, "Meg, try and get some sleep tonight, you'll need your strength." He grinned and hung up the phone, winking at her through the window as he walked past.

A tired James arrived at Meghan's at ten minutes past six the following morning, his exhaustion forgotten when Meghan opened the door in her robe, ushering him in and flinging it off, revealing her perfect naked body underneath. Laughing at his shock, she slowly undid the buttons on his shirt, removing it and adding it to her gown on the floor, kissing him deeply, her breasts brushing against his firm chest. Taking his hand in hers, she led him through to the bathroom and started the shower, stepping under the water while he removed his pants and shoes, kicking them aside before stepping in next to her. His arms encircled her waist from behind, and she felt his erection against her buttocks, smiling with delight at his need for her. She turned in his arms, picking up the condom she left on the edge of the sink and unwrapping it, sliding it down his length while his mouth found hers, hungrily tasting her, drinking her in. His hands cupped her buttocks, lifting her up, and she wrapped her legs around his waist, settling herself onto his erection. He tethered her against the shower wall, hands holding her hips steady as he plunged in and out of her in a frantic rhythm that had them both frantic with need. James screamed her name as he came, anchoring her against his length as he pulsed inside of her. Feeling his release seeping through her core was Meghan's undoing, and she screamed out his name, clamping down on his shoulder as lust overtook her senses.

With unsteady legs they stumbled from the shower and across to Meghan's bed, neither one wanting to take their hands off the other, starved of each other's touch over the past few days. The spell they had managed to wrap themselves in was broken shortly after noon of the following day, with James's pager bleeping out an emergency code. They laughed and agreed that a day off didn't actually exist. Dressing in record speed, he kissed Meghan longingly, promised to talk to her later, and rushed home to change into his Royal Flying Doctor Service retrieval flight uniform of navy-blue cargo pants and a matching long-sleeved button-down shirt. Within forty minutes of being paged James was in the retrieval car headed to the Royal Flying Doctor Service hangar where a fixed-wing aircraft was fuelled and waiting to take him to Finke, approximately an hour's flight out of Alice Springs, dependant on the weather and any possible turbulence. James hoped there wouldn't be any delays on this flight today, they were on their way to a motor vehicle accident, and early reports from the local police at Finke suggested that a single-car, speeding heavily, had ploughed into a grove of trees. The sedan was overcrowded, carrying twelve people instead of the legally allowed five people, and James had been told that five of the passengers were children, and none of them had been wearing seatbelts.

On the flight to Finke, further information came in, advising James that two of the passengers, both children aged under five, had been pronounced deceased at the scene by local law enforcement officers, and an earlier Royal Flying Doctor Service retrieval team that had been dispatched had requested that a further team be sent for support. Once landed, James met up with the first retrieval team on the scene, and together they worked nonstop throughout the afternoon, treating and stabilising patients. Six of the adults were very lucky to suffer only minor injuries, lacerations and a few broken bones, and they were discharged from the care of the Royal Flying Doctor Service and referred to the local Finke clinic for treatment; which allowed James and Michelle, the other flight doctor on the scene, to concentrate on the more serious patients. Despite their best efforts, James and Michelle were unable to save the life of a baby boy and sorrowfully handed him over to the local law enforcement officers for transport into the Finke clinic. As dusk was starting to fall, James and Michelle loaded the remaining adult and two children into the Royal Flying Doctor Service aircraft in preparation for transfer back to Alice Springs hospital.

It was close to midnight when James had finally finished his paperwork and clocked off, and he took a seat in the staff lounge room and took out his mobile intending to call Meghan, surprised instead to find a text from her, sent not long after he had left her house earlier that day.

Erica is sick, I've been called into work. Talk tomorrow x

James smiled as he jogged down the steps from the Alice Springs Emergency Department, taking them two at a time. He swiped his access card at the main entrance and walked the short distance to the children's ward, again swiping his access card to gain access to the secure ward. As a doctor, he wasn't questioned or stopped as he walked through the ward to the nurses' station. He took a moment to surreptitiously watch Meghan through the glass partition of the nurses' station as she moved around inside, before moving to lean in the doorway and knocking gently on the window.

"James!" Her hand flew to her heart. "You scared me witless! Are you okay? When did you get back?"

"Just now," his eyes drank her in, it felt like days since he had last seen her, instead of only hours. "When do you finish?"

"In about half an hour, maybe a little earlier depending on how long handover takes. Why?" she raised an eyebrow at him. "Was there something you wanted?" she teased, slowly looking him up and down, a smile curling her lip.

"I'm finished for the night; I can wait here until your shift ends if you like? You know, if that won't be too distracting for you." Meghan loved the way his eyes crinkled up at the corners when he smiled.

"I'm sure I'll manage," Meghan quipped. They spoke of mundane things, Meghan discovering that James had four older sisters, despised green beans, and had a fascination for reality TV shows such as "Extreme Emergency" and "Ambulance".

"Seriously," Meghan laughed, "don't you get enough of that type of drama at work?" James in turn found it astonishing that Meghan hated being on the ocean and teased her about literally being the only person he had ever met who did not like ice cream, jelly, pancakes or custard.

Time flew past and with the handover done, Meghan out of the door with a smile.

"You know what I was thinking," James started, slinging his arm around Meghan's shoulders and tucking her into his side, leading her down the corridor and around the corner, headed towards the staff exit door that would take them out to the accommodation blocks and to his Waratah unit.

"I can only imagine." Meghan raised an eyebrow at him and the direction he was leading them in but didn't question it, watching a lazy grin appear on his face.

"Actually..." James drawled, "I was thinking that we should have dinner. Tonight." He stopped in front of the locked exit door, swiping his access card to release it.

"James, I can't, I'm completely exhausted," Meghan apologised, disappointment colouring her reply, earning a hearty laugh from James.

"Dinner Meg, that's all. Well, dinner and bed. To sleep," he added quickly, "nothing else. I promise," he placed his hand over his heart in a mock boy scout salute, not at all convincing, "I will even cook for you this time," he grinned at her.

"Really?" Meghan's interest was piqued, she couldn't remember the last time anyone had cooked for her. "That actually sounds really nice."

They finished the short stroll to his apartment in relative silence, broken only by Meghan's frightened gasp and James's rich laugh as she jumped behind him, clinging to his arm. "Sorry," Meghan was glad of the darkness to hide her flaming cheeks. "I don't, um, really like lizards."

"So I see," James grinned into the dark, enjoying the way Meghan clung to him for support. "I promise, no lizards will hurt you on my watch," he joked, earning a soft punch in the arm from Meghan, who didn't let go of his arm until they were safely inside his apartment. Meghan watched him from her perch at the breakfast bar, as he foraged through the fridge, pulling out a selection of ingredients and getting to work on making them both some dinner. He sliced the tomato with a concentration that made Meghan laugh, and placed it on top of the ham and cheese, closing the lids of both of the sandwiches and then placing them on the grill to toast. She caught hold of the front of his flight shirt as he moved past her, drawing him into a soft kiss. He looked more than tired, Meghan thought there was a distraction about him tonight, that maybe his mind was somewhere else. It wasn't until after they had finished their toasted sandwiches, tidied up the kitchen, and were both in bed that he told her what was on her mind.

Wrapped tightly in Meghan's arms, James spoke softly into the still of the darkness. "I lost a patient today, a toddler."

"Oh, James," Meghan's heart lurched, and she wrapped her arms tighter still around his chest, holding him close.

"There are two more small children up in intensive care, battling to survive, all because of their bad luck at having irresponsible, ignorant parents," he fumed.

"When I have children there is no way I will ever put them in danger, no way I don't fight to protect them, whatever the cost." Meghan's blood ran cold. There it was, the reminder she knew would eventually come, the reason she would never belong in James's life, even if she wanted to. Meghan knew that they were never going to be anything but casual acquaintances, a distant memory to look back on when they were both old and grey. It was a reality that kept her awake long after James had fallen asleep, breathing softly, his limbs entwined with hers. She knew that she would have to tell him, that she couldn't keep her secret from him forever, but being the coward that she was, she knew she would wait just a little bit longer. After his contract was up, she promised herself, she would tell him. After all, it was only another month or so, what harm would it do.

When Meghan awoke it was to find that James was already gone. Padding into the bathroom she showered quickly and dressed in yesterday's clothes, making a feeble attempt at smoothing out the wrinkles in her dress before, feeling more human, she went to look for James. She found him hunched over the kitchen breakfast bar, in the middle of what looked like a deep discussion with Matt and another male, whose face she recognised from their brief meeting outside of the hospital kitchen the other day, all looking engrossed at something on his laptop screen. Catching sight of her hovering in the doorway, James smiled. "Good morning, well, good afternoon actually," James crossed to kiss her, glancing at the clock above the fridge, placing a hand on the small of her back and guiding her to the spare stool at the breakfast bar. "Coffee?" Meghan smiled and nodded, not sure she could speak, feeling rather like a bug under a microscope. By the way, his friends were looking at her, it was pretty clear that James hadn't told them that Meghan was here. As awkward as it was, James had told Meghan that he would be discreet, and she felt a giddy wave of happiness well up inside her at the knowledge that he had kept his word to her.

"Guys, seriously, stop staring at her," James's exasperated voice came from across the room as he crossed to place a coffee in front of Meghan, slinging an arm across her shoulders and leaving it there. "It's weird."

"Sorry, Meghan." Matthew apologised. "We didn't realise you were here, or we would have caught up with James later." He shot James a pointed glare of reprimand.

"Yeah James, you should have told us you had more important things to, uh, do."

"Xavier," James and Matt chorused a warning in unison. While they were well versed in Xavier's unique and oftentimes juvenile sense of humour, it was not something that most women, or anyone actually, ever appreciated.

"I'm Xavier," he extended his hand to Meghan. "We only rib him because we are happy for him, he never brings anyone home," he confessed to her in a conspiratorial whisper, shooting her a wink, causing her to smile. He might be a big charmer, but there was something genuine that Meghan saw was lurking underneath. By the way, the three friends spoke to each other, Meghan could see that there was a long history there, mutual respect, and a strong friendship.

"Interesting," she raised her eyebrows at James, knowing that Xavier's statement was true by the way he shifted uncomfortably. So James didn't make it a habit to bring women back to his place, the knowledge sent a deliciously warm shiver curling through Meghan. Huh, Meghan would have thought that bringing women home would have been a pretty regular occurrence for James if she was honest, especially considering how insatiable James seemed to be when he was with her. Hiding her snort of surprise by taking a large swig of coffee, Meghan gestured towards the laptop, asking "So, what is it that has you all concentrating so hard on your day off?"

"My parents are hosting a party for their wedding anniversary at the end of the month, and we are trying to find the perfect gift to send them," James answered matter of fact.

"You know the end of the month is only two weeks away, right?" Meghan checked with them.

"Yes, which is part of our problem," James grinned sheepishly at her. "We sort of forgot. I bet you are one of those super organised people who finishes all of your gift shopping months in advance, aren't you?" he guessed. "What did you get for your parent's anniversary?"

"Actually, no." Meghan drew a deep breath, correcting him quietly. "My parents are dead, they died when I was a child," she continued flatly.

"Oh God, Meg, I'm sorry," James squeezed her hand instinctively.

"It's fine," she shrugged, the words sounding hollow even to her own ears.

"I guess we could always send them a gift voucher," mused Matthew, scrolling down the page and not seeing anything that he particularly liked.

"Are you all working for the rest of the month?" Meghan was curious to know. Seeing them all shake their heads in the negative, she asked "Why don't you just go home for their anniversary party and surprise them? I am sure they would much rather have you with them, instead of any gift." I know I would, the thought popped unbidden into her head and she carefully avoided James's gaze so that he wouldn't be able to guess what it was that she was thinking.

"Are you working for the rest of the month Meg?" James changed the subject, distracting her.

"More than likely," she shrugged. "I tend to do more unplanned overtime and midnight shifts than most of the other staff. I'm the only one who, um, doesn't have anyone waiting at home. It is easy for me to be able to cover staff sick leave and public holidays," she cleared her throat self-consciously, aware of James staring at her intently. "It's not so bad, most of the staff are cheery enough, and I am happy to do it. Besides, holidays are a time for those with family to be with them, making memories."

"The three of us always share holidays together," Xavier spoke, clearing the underlying tension in the room. "It has been our tradition since university, we all have large families, so they never miss us. No matter where we are all working, we always meet up. This year, we plan to celebrate here."

"Here," Meghan looked around James's apartment dubiously. "You don't even have a dining table."

"I'll get one soon," James held up his hands in mock surrender. "I've just been a bit busy lately." The way he looked at Meghan as he said it left no one in any doubt as to his meaning of the word busy and sent shivers down her spine. With a pointed look at each other, Xavier and Matthew made a hasty exit, professing they had a long list of things to do, and promising to talk to James later

The door had barely closed before James claimed her mouth with an intensity that left her hungry for more. Groaning impatiently with need into her mouth, James was surprised when she pulled away from him. Taking his hand, she led him back through the unit, into his bedroom in silence, pulling his shirt over his head and making quick work of his jeans and boxer shorts until he stood, naked, in front of her.

"Your turn," he growled, removing her already wrinkled dress, undoing her bra, and letting her breasts spring free. Capturing one of her pink nipples in his mouth, he bent her backwards, cupping her buttocks in his other hand, holding her flush to his erection. It stunned him, his attraction to her, his primal need to have her, the way a single look from her had him coming undone. He slid his hand to the front of her panties, pushing the thin fabric aside and plunging a finger deep into her core, rewarded with her excited moan and an unexpected buck of her hips. He slid his finger in and out of her, enjoying the feeling of her becoming wetter and wetter under his ministrations until his need for her became more pressing, and he pulled back, bending to strip her of her panties and, arm around her waist, drew her down on to his bed.

Meghan giggled delightedly as he landed atop of her, the thick head of his erection nudging her sensitive nub. She reached her hands up and guided his mouth back down to her nipples, relishing the sensations he elicited from her. Sighing with contentment, she rolled them over, surprising James by straddling him and giving him a delicious view of her heavy breasts. Smiling lazily, she leant over his chiselled chest to kiss him deeply, her nipples grazing against his firm chest. His hands glided down her sides, cupping her bottom and pressing her firmly against his erection. Meghan moved her hips in small circles as she deepened the kiss, her nub rubbing against James's hard length, teasing him slowly, gasping and jerking away from his mouth when his hand slipped in between them and gave her nub a hard tweak, shooting spasms of pleasure to her very core. Straightening up, with James's hand still kneading and rolling her nub between his fingers, Meghan took a condom from the dresser and unwrapped it, rolling it down James's shaft, then, with a wink, she grasped James's erection, using her hand to guide his throbbing length deep inside of her aching centre. James watched in fascination as Meghan slowly slid down the length of his shaft, almost all the way, and then slid back up again, torturously slowly, with a wicked smile on her gorgeous face.

Desperate with need and unable to stand the wait any longer, James released her nub, before reaching up and grabbing hold of her hips, pulling her all the way down on his shaft in one swift move, drawing a surprised gasp from Meghan's parted lips. James nearly came undone as he watched his shaft disappear completely into Meghan's centre, feeling her muscles stretch to accommodate his size. She was mesmerising, he decided as he watched her arch her back, flinging her head back as she sang his name, taking him deeper still. He started to move inside her, his eyes feasting on the sight of her, hypnotised by the way her breasts swayed and danced for him as she met and rode every one of his thrusts, the way she threw her head back in a scream of triumph as she orgasmed atop of him, bucking her hips as her release tore through her. Gripping his hips, Meghan called his name, tipping him over the edge and grinding down onto him until his spasms stopped, collapsing onto his chest with a contented sigh. James had never been more spent in his life, or more turned on. Being with Meghan was a heady experience that he was fast becoming addicted to, with her, everything just felt right, even the way her luscious breasts currently felt against his chiselled chest was exactly as it should be.

Holding her in his arms, lightly stroking her back, James spoke without thought. "You were right about my parent's anniversary. I should go home, especially this year. My parents are hosting it at their property up near Tennant Creek, and all four of my sisters and their families will be there. It would be nice to see everyone. I know this might seem pretty crazy Meg," James continued, "but why don't you come home with me?"

"What?!" Meghan's head snapped upwards. James was just as surprised as Meghan at his invitation and had no idea what had possessed him to invite her. Selfish reasons maybe, he mused internally. After all, they had only been lovers for a few weeks, which was certainly not enough time to get to know someone, and yet...He felt completely at ease with her, more so than he had ever felt with Jessinta, which was certainly a revelation he wasn't expecting to have. "Come home with me," he repeated firmly, warming up to the idea the more he thought about it. "It will be fun. We can stay in one of my parent's guest cottages, and my sisters will all be there with their brood of terrors to entertain us," he smiled at the thought.

"James, I can't," Meghan pushed herself to a sitting position atop James, who tried to remain focused on what she was saying, now was not the time to be thinking about the way her fingers felt against the sides of his groin.

"We agreed that this thing between us would be kept casual," her voice held a warning. "We agreed that neither one of us wants a relationship. Going home with you for your parent's anniversary would change that, our whole dynamic would shift, whether you think so or not. Tell me honestly, have you changed your mind?" James was quiet for a moment, thinking the question through, wanting to be as honest with her as he could be.

"No, I haven't changed my mind," he answered honestly. "I am not looking for a relationship, despite the fact that you turn me on in a way that no other woman ever has, Meg," he smiled up at her. "Selfishly I want to have you with me. I want to wake up with you wrapped around me, if you'll let me, and see what happens." Meghan knew that she should say no, she knew that she was torturing herself by even contemplating agreeing to his crazy idea, and yet…She was tempted, so very tempted. She longed to feel like she was a part of a family again, to spend time with James, to pretend that they were a normal couple, to pretend that they were in a relationship. She had to say no though, she couldn't do it, it would hurt her way too much when he found out the truth about her, and that was something that she just could not risk happening. She had to end it, now, before things got even further complicated.

This is why she was so surprised when she opened her mouth and replied "Okay James, I'll go home with you."

James called his parents while Meghan was in the shower, letting them know that he would be home for their party and that he was bringing a friend with him.

"A friend," his mother sounded way too excited about the prospect James realised with a weary sigh. "A female friend?"

"Yes mum, Meghan. I think you'll like her, she's a nurse at the hospital." He could almost hear the wheels turning in his mother's head. "Can we stay in the cabins? I was thinking maybe Blaze and Star?" he continued.

"Yes, yes, of course, you can. I'll have the girls help me get them ready. It's so exciting!"

"No fuss, okay mum? We really are just friends." James tried again, rolling his eyes.

"Of course you are dear," his mother placated. "I understand." James groaned inwardly. He shuddered to think what would await them when they arrived. His parents, Jenny and Chris, had owned The

Speckled Star, a working cattle station that ran camps, pony clubs, and farm stay vacations, for fifteen years. Outside of their children and grandchildren, it was their greatest pride.

James watched as Meghan dressed, feeling rather reluctant to let her leave, and attempted to entice her into staying for dinner, but she refused, telling him that if he intended to whisk her away for a week, then he would have to let her go home and get organised. She had work in a few hours, not to mention the fact that she needed to find someone to cover her while she was away. "Besides," she dropped a kiss onto his cheek, "you also need to get ready. I suspect that Matt and Xavier would prefer it if you were actually dressed when they arrive for dinner." Knowing that she was right, he let her go, with the promise of seeing her again tomorrow.

James could see the disappointment that Matthew and Xavier tried to hide when he told them of his decision to return to Tennant Creek and attend his parents' anniversary party. He had deliberately waited until the end of the meal before he broached the subject with them, hoping that the seafood and beer would have mellowed them out somewhat. As he started to explain the sudden change of plans and how they came to be, he was interrupted by a knock at the door. Crossing to open it, he found Meghan standing there brandishing a pavlova, wearing a rather guilty look on her face. "Dessert," she announced, kissing his cheek and then stepping past him to walk through and place it on the breakfast bar. "I was thinking about what you were saying earlier, about your tradition of having holidays together," she addressed Xavier and Matthew, "and I was thinking, why don't the two of you just drive down to The Speckled Star as well? Then that way you and James can still have your tradition," she beamed at them. And I won't be alone with him in a family setting, she added silently to herself, feeling the familiar doubts already starting to creep in and having her second guess her decision in agreeing to go with him. "I'll leave you guys to discuss it,

I have to get to work." She kissed James softly on the cheek and headed out.

Meghan hoped that the next couple of weeks would pass quickly. She was nervous at the prospect of going away with James and knew that the more time she had to herself, the more she would be able to second guess her decision and try to talk herself into changing her mind.

CHAPTER SEVEN

Meghan was almost due to finish her shift, rather slow for a Saturday night when the call came in. The hospital was enacting a Code Brown, their internal emergency. There had been a horrific accident at a popular car race, heavily populated with both locals and tourists. One of the propane tanks on the cars had exploded, sending a fireball ripping through the stands of spectators. The consultants from each of the hospital departments had been called in, as well as their senior staff members, extra doctors for the emergency department, and the teams of retrieval doctors, the Royal Flying Doctor Service aircraft already being prepared for take-off at the hangar. All the staff knew so far was that eight patients were currently being transported to the hospital via ambulance, with a further twenty-two injured en route via private vehicles. At least three children were among the victims. The staff on the children's ward rushed around relocating patients into shared rooms, freeing up and prepping the critical care rooms. Staff due to finish were preparing to stay indefinitely and extra staff were being called in. Meghan knew they were in for a busy night.

The first patient arrived in a rush of beeping machines and medical jargon, underlined by the cries of relatives. Meghan donned gloves and peeled the bright coloured sticker off of the trauma chart, attaching it to the front of her uniform. She was on resus and airways tonight. Meghan's heart sank when she saw just how bad the injuries were.

"This is Leethan, a 3-year-old male, with burns to 80 per cent of his body." Meghan's eyes shot up to meet James's, she knew what that statistic meant.

"Stabilise and transport?" She stood back as Leethan was transferred from the ambulance gurney onto a hospital bed.

"No, transport is not a viable option for this patient."

"What?! You can't be serious?"

"Nurse!" James snapped, already tired of this fight. "A word outside please." Nodding sharply, Meghan brushed past James into the hallway.

"What the hell Meghan?"

"I'm sorry, I should never have questioned you in front of everyone else, but James, you and I both know that if Leethan is not transported to an interstate burns unit he will be lucky to survive the night."

"He would be lucky to survive the trip out to the hangar. Look, we have dozens more patients that could benefit from being transferred to the burn units Meghan, I'm sorry, but Leethan isn't one of them."

"James! Shame on you." Meghan shook her head sadly. "People pull through all the time, even when the odds are stacked against them. If he stabilises, will you transport him?"

"Meghan," James touched her cheek briefly, "don't get your hopes up, please?"

"Will you?" Meghan persisted.

"If he stabilises for longer than six hours, I will talk to the director about a transfer."

Leethan Dixon stopped breathing precisely three hours later. Meghan activated the Code Blue alarm, dropping the rails on the bed and beginning CPR, climbing up next to Leethan to get better leverage. She continued chest compressions as the Medical Emergency Team assessed Leethan around her. The rush of activity stopped, and the room fell silent, the only sound the soft counting as Meghan pumped Leethan's chest.

"Time of death 11:59 pm. Meghan, stop, he's gone." James wasn't sure Meghan had heard him and was about to speak again when she suddenly moved, climbing down off the bed and looking at him.

"You did this." She turned and left the room, there were other patients she had to help, and if she had to look at James right now she would say something that she would regret, she just knew it.

Meghan watched through the glass partition as James told Leethan's parents, saw his mother crumble, and his father shout out in denial. She saw as Leethan's grieving parents were swept along by a sea of relatives, all wailing as one. The wails coming from his indigenous family were piercing, they tore through the toughest of resolve. It was an eerie mix of song and despair, and Meghan knew that it would be ceaseless for several days, constantly changing as new family members joined in the mourning and others returned to their own families, as was their custom. Sensing he was being watched, James turned, finding Meghan staring at him. With a sigh, he moved toward her. Walking into the room, James closed the blinds across the glass partition and drew Meghan's stiff form into his arms. "You should have taken him straight to Adelaide."

"Meg," James's voice was defeated, "it wasn't my call." If only she knew. James was the one who initially assessed Leethan, he knew the only chance of survival was evacuation to Adelaide hospital, which had a world-class burns unit there. He had made his case to Michelle, Director of Air Medical Services, and had been refused.

"I have to go back to work." She pulled away from James, feeling suddenly very tired. It was on days like this that she wondered if she was making any difference at all, being a nurse.

"Will I see you later?" There was a tentativeness in James's voice, and Meghan softened.

"James," she placed a soft hand on James's cheek. "Yes. I may be upset and disappointed, but that is work us, not private us." She offered up a small smile, before turning and leaving.

The incident with Leethan had rattled Meghan, and when James arrived at her house shortly before dawn, she was waiting, buzzing with a raw need. Meghan jerked the door open as he reached the landing, desire blazing in her eyes. James closed the distance between them and claimed her mouth with a hard kiss, kicking the door shut behind him. There were no sweet words, no teasing touches, only a raw need. James spun with Meghan in his arms, pushing her up against the back of the front door. His hands sought out the hem of her dress, breaking their kiss momentarily to rip it up and over her head, throwing it on the floor beside them. Meghan fumbled with the buttons on his jeans, pushing them down to his knees along with his boxer shorts. He was already rock hard, bulging. He ached for her. In one fluid movement, James drew one of Meghan's legs up to his waist, his fingers pushed her panties to the side, and he plunged into her moistness with a grunt.

He angled her hips, withdrawing his length and plunging inside again, deeper and deeper, increasing his speed with each thrust. He knew she was close; he saw it in her eyes as his length plundered as deep inside her as was physically possible. With a final twitch, he tipped her over the edge. Her eyes wide, Meghan clawed at his chest, panting fast, dripping with need, lost in screams of pleasure and the heady scent of lust. Watching her come undone was all that James needed, and with a triumphant shout, his orgasm ripped through him. They clung to each other, not daring to move until their breathing returned to normal.

"Hi," James grinned down at a dishevelled Meghan.

"Hi yourself," Meghan blushed, embarrassed, never having allowed herself to give so fully to a lover before. "Bed?"

James tipped back his head and laughed, scooping her up into his arms and carrying her into the bedroom. Setting her at the foot of the bed, he slipped out of his shirt, kicking his trousers and boxers off and adding them to the pile. Once naked, he stepped forward, cupping Meghan's breasts and kneading them through her lacy bra, watching them peak under his intense gaze. Bowing his head to capture her nipple, he sucks hard, eliciting a gasp from Meghan, the lacy confines increasing the sensations. Reaching behind her, James unclipped her bra, Meghan's breasts bouncing free, begging to be touched. His tongue darted out, flicking across her hardened nipple, suckling and nipping at it with his teeth. His hand trailed down to her panties, wet to the touch. He knew if he slid two fingers inside her silky folds, he would feel her pool of wetness wrap around him. Instead, he fell to his knees, sliding her panties slowly downwards, until they were free of her legs.

He leant forwards, tasting her wetness, tongue probing her core, her eyes round as she watched him.

James could feel Meghan writhing against his mouth, trying to get closer, whimpering with need. Knowing she was ready for him, he guided her to sit on the edge of the bed, lifting her knees up and over his shoulders, giving him a perfect view of her silky folds. Knowing that he was responsible for her obvious wetness only highlighted his ache, his member growing uncomfortable, making his need even more urgent. With a low groan, James dipped his head, tongue plunging deep inside, tasting Meghan's delicate folds. Meghan fevered with delight, encouraging him, James's hard length shuddering in anticipation as she sighed his name, reaching between them to grip his shaft tightly in her hand. Straightening up, James captures her hand in his own, guiding it up over her head, holding it there. With a single thrust, his thick shaft enters deep into her softness, her walls stretching to accommodate his length with a delighted shout from Meghan.

His need urgent, James increases the rhythm of his thrusts, faster and faster, relishing the feel of Meghan moving in sync against him, thrusting her hips to take him deeper inside her centre. James moves faster, so close to his release, Meghan moaning and screaming out his name. their release is mutual, Meghan gripping James's shoulders, shudders echoing through her body as he emptied his need deep inside of her, filling her, before collapsing atop her on the bed. Meghan wasn't sure how long they stayed this way, her fingers dancing across James's chest and over his shaft, already starting to stir. She delighted in the knowledge that he was insatiable, and wondered if she would ever tire of him, of having him buried deep inside of her, feeling her body wrap around his so perfectly? For now, comfort had been found, and given. The disappointment and sadness of the day were forgotten.

Meghan was out of sorts throughout her shift, there was a restlessness about her that didn't go unnoticed by the rest of the staff, Tessa drawing her aside and asking her outright if there was anything wrong.

"You were right, about James," Meghan started, "we have started seeing each other for a few weeks now, nothing serious," she hastened to add before Tessa got too excited for her. "We are keeping it casual, neither one of us is looking for anything serious. Anyway, James's family own The Speckled Star up near Tennant Creek, and he has invited me to join them for a week. We are leaving tomorrow, I'm sorry I didn't say anything, I wasn't quite sure how to bring it up."

"You're kidding," Tessa gasped. "That's huge!" She was practically thrumming with excitement, and Meghan shushed her frantically, hoping that no one else had overheard their conversation.

"Please don't tell anyone," she begged. "It's a one-off thing, he's only here for a few more months, and anyway, I'm not his type." Meghan finished in a rush.

Tessa assured Meghan that she wouldn't breathe a word of her secret to anyone, and sure of her discretion, Meghan and Tessa spent the rest of their shift in companionable conversation. James phoned the ward shortly before the end of Meghan's shift to let her know that he had been called out on a retrieval and was fully expecting to have to transport the patients directly to Melbourne, and therefore most likely wouldn't be back in Alice Springs until late tomorrow afternoon. Meghan told him not to worry and assured him that she would be packed and ready to leave as soon as he was back in town. Considering that she had yet to start packing her bag, she only hoped that would prove to be true. As it happened, James called her shortly after she arrived home, to let her know that his patient had passed away before the Royal Flying Doctor Service aircraft had left the runway, and the retrieval had been called off. He was going to use this time to his advantage and head into town to shop for an anniversary present for his parents if she wanted to join him?

"You still don't know what to get your mum, do you," Meghan teased, her suspicions confirmed by James's helpless groan.

"I have some ideas," he argued, "I would just prefer to get your opinion first," he admitted. "Please? It will be fun...Maybe." James wasn't convinced. Neither was Meghan, who highly doubted that a trip into the Alice Springs shopping precinct, at this hour of the day, with school already out and harried mothers ushering tired children through the never-ending checkout line would be anything like fun. However, she found herself agreeing to be picked up in twenty minutes, and surprisingly looking forward to it. Being peak hour, Meghan doubted they would find a parking space, raising an eyebrow sceptically at James as he pulled into a spot marked 'reserved', located behind the popular medical clinic situated directly opposite the one and only shopping centre in the middle of town.

"I do a shift here once a month," he shrugged by way of explanation, "this is my spot. It seems silly to just have it sit here empty, so I use it whenever I have to come into town." James captured Meghan's hand in his own, lacing his fingers with hers, smiling when she made no attempt to remove it.

"Where to first?" Meghan asked as they made their way across the road towards the shopping centre. "I thought I would try the jewellery shop, mum has quite the collection of crystal ornaments, and I think they sell some of them there, but first," he steered her in a beeline towards the one and only fresh fruit juice shop, "what will you have?" James insisted on paying for their drinks, his watermelon, celery and guava concoction, and her apple and pineapple freeze, silencing Meghan's protests with a kiss. As they waited for their drinks to be made, James was greeted by a colleague who Meghan didn't recognise, the other woman's curiosity in her was obvious by the way she continued to stare at Meghan, despite the fact that James made no move to introduce them. Meghan had never been more relieved to have her order ready, not at all comfortable with being scrutinised. With drinks in hand, James excused them.

"Well, that was incredibly awkward," Meghan's catty tone told James what he had suspected, he should have introduced her.

"Meg, she is just a colleague," he tried to placate her.

"Do you think I care about her? James, you are free to see whoever you want," Meghan shrugged. "The issue is, this is a small town, people will talk, she will probably race back to the hospital telling everyone, and before you know it – wham! The whole place will know, which will be pretty awkward for me once you move on."

"Meg," James threw back his head and laughed. "I thought...Actually never mind what I thought. I'm sorry, next time we see someone else we know we shall duck behind the largest person we see and hope that they block us from view." He was so close to telling her that he had actually thought that she was jealous of his colleague, which was ridiculous, Meghan had no need to worry, casual or not, James was a gentleman and would never see two women at once. He felt almost deflated that she hadn't been jealous and shook his head to clear the thought, tired, that was the problem, he was just tired.

"There are so many pretty ones, how will you choose?" standing in front of the jeweller's window with James felt cosy, and way too comfortable for Meghan. She knew that they looked like a proper couple, with his hand entwined with hers, and while they had been standing here looking in the window, they had attracted more than a few passing glances and knowing smiles. Oh, dear. Unsure if James had noticed them or not, Meghan decided not to mention them, if they didn't bother him, she wouldn't let them bother her either.

"Honestly, I am not sure I can even remember which ones she doesn't have anymore. Which one would you choose?"

"The octopus," Meghan answered without pause. "It is nice to have a reminder of the ocean when you live in the desert." In the end, James purchased three, the octopus, a small deer, and a rose in a bud vase.

"Meghan," a larger woman passing by stopped to envelope Meghan in a warm hug. "I am so glad I ran into you!" The woman gave James a thorough scrutinising, all the while keeping up a fast-flowing conversation with Meghan. As the lady kept up her friendly chatter with Meghan, James happily eavesdropped, not at all embarrassed to be actively listening in, the woman obviously thought that he and Meghan were close friends and he felt no need to correct her. By the time they had made it back to Meghan's house, the stop-start of the flow of the traffic and the bright glare of the high beams on the passing cars had all combined to give Meghan the start of a migraine, something she suffered from viciously yet infrequently. Assuring James that she would take some paracetamol and head straight to bed and that she would still be fine to leave as planned the following day, she kissed him lightly goodnight and carried her bags inside, leaving them on the kitchen table, more tired than she had ever remembered feeling before. She took the paracetamol, kicked off her shoes and crawled into bed fully clothed, sound asleep by half-past seven.

God her head was throbbing! The banging was getting louder and louder, and unable to stand it anymore, Meghan sat up in her bed, tangled in a mess of sheets and pillows, momentarily disorientated. The banging was incessant, breaking through the fog of Meghan's half-asleep state. The door, someone was at the door. Meghan staggered down the hall and looked through the brass peephole. James. Meghan opened the door, squinting up at him. "What time is it?" she croaked.

"Shit, Meghan, you look awful!" Letting himself inside, James shut and locked the door, leading Meghan by the arm back to her bedroom. "Here," he pushed her back down onto the bed, straightening the tangled sheets and pulling them up over her, checking her forehead with the back of his hand. "You don't have a temperature, which is good," he commented.

"Migraine," Meghan groaned, closing her eyes on the image of James's face, which struck her as almost looking concerned. She felt the bed move as he stood to leave, unsure why it annoyed her so much that he was leaving. She knew their relationship was purely physical, and if she thought about it, she wasn't sure she would want him there anyway, not while she was so sick and looking like hell. But still…She had always been overly needy when she was ill, that must be what it was, she decided, drifting back to sleep.

When Meghan woke again the room was pitch black. Rolling over she collided with something hard and warm, and very much naked. James. He stayed, her heart skipped a beat, she didn't know if she was annoyed or not with this discovery.

"Of course, I stayed, I couldn't exactly leave you to fend for yourself now, could I?" James's voice startled Meghan, she hadn't realised that she had spoken out loud and cringed. "Now, stop overthinking whatever it is you are overthinking and lay back down," he ordered. Flopping back against the pillows, Meghan couldn't switch her thoughts off. James had stayed, even though she was sick, a new experience for Meghan and something she wasn't used to. She wasn't sure that she wanted to get used to it either, becoming familiar with James would only end in heartbreak, of that she was certain. After all, hadn't they agreed to a no strings attached fling? James sighed heavily and drew her into his arms. "Why are you still thinking?"

"Sorry, I can't help it, now that I am awake there is so much that I need to do." Turning on the bedside light, Meghan studied James. He looked worn out, stretched out on his side, looking back at her. "Go back to sleep," Meghan cupped his face, kissing him gently. "I'm just going to potter around and pack so we can still leave on time."

With her migraine gone, Meghan made herself a strong black coffee and took it through to the spare room, her own bedroom being too small to house a wardrobe. She pulled down her suitcase and started throwing a random assortment of outfits in, not quite sure what she would be needing. Meghan was very much a dress person, preferring them over any other type of clothing, no matter what season it was, and it took some time for her to locate a pair of jeans, throwing them in just in case they were needed. She added a few cosmetics in case she decided to dress up, her toiletries, and spying them on the bathroom shelf, her sanitary items, knowing that they would be needed. Once she had packed, Meghan did a load of washing, gave the kitchen floor a quick mop, and then ducked out to the supermarket to pick up a few groceries for Tessa, who would be house-sitting while Meghan was away. She returned to find James already up, showered and dressed, looking as sexy as hell, waiting for her. Tessa arrived on time and James waited tactfully in the car while Meghan said goodbye to Tessa, with Tessa squeezing her and reminding her to just have fun. As they left the township of Alice Springs behind, Meghan's excitement grew at the adventure ahead.

The drive was uneventful, James and Meghan broke up the monotony of the dry barren landscape by playing carpool karaoke, and insane eye spy. Halfway between the barely-there town of Ti Tree and Tennant Creek, James found a spot for them to pull off, declaring himself starving, and reaching for the picnic blanket and food that Meghan had packed in the car earlier. They walked a short distance until they found a shady spot not too far from the road, and James did a quick check before laying the blanket down, not wanting to disturb anything slithery.

"You did tell your parents that I am coming with you, didn't you?" Meghan checked again, for the zillionth time since James had first invited her along.

"Of course I did," James sounded surprised at her question. "You don't have to worry Meg, they are fine with it." In actual fact they had been more than fine, they had been beside themselves with glee, convinced that James had finally moved on from Jessinta, a fact that James decided would be best kept from Meghan. Remembering how happy they had been when he mentioned Meghan made James feel more than a bit guilty, it wasn't that he had lied exactly, he just hadn't been entirely truthful with his parents, a situation that didn't sit very easily with him.

"What did you tell them exactly, about who I was, and why I was coming with you?" Meghan squinted her eyes at him, and he tried not to squirm under the scrutiny.

"I told them that we are work colleagues, which is technically true."

"James! They are probably expecting me to be a doctor or a flight nurse, not someone who is just working in the children's ward," Meghan gaped at him, horrified. How on earth did he think that she would be able to pull off a ruse like that? The most that she knew of the Royal Flying Doctor Service and how they operated was the scant information she had gleaned from touring their local base, and that was years ago now, when she had first arrived in town.

"What would you rather I had told them?" His eyebrows raised. "That we are lovers? That we are not in a relationship, that what we have it is purely sex?" He couldn't resist teasing her a little bit.

"No!" Meghan looked mortified at the thought. "Colleagues is fine," she finished lamely, munching on her apple. "So, is there anything I need to know before I meet your family?"

"My dad, Gerhardus, was an engineer, and my mother, Zonja, was a school teacher," James stated matter of factly. "Then when they moved to Australia, their qualifications weren't recognised, so they bought the cattle station and have poured everything they have into making it a success. You know I have four older sisters, Arabella, Elspeth, Lusea, and Fleur; we were all born in South Africa and emigrated here when I was eleven. They are all married, with thirteen children between them so far, ranging in age from ten years down to six months." James took a swig of water and contemplated how much more to tell Meghan.

"Let me guess, they are so used to you bringing home "work colleagues"," she used air quotations, much to James's amusement, "that they won't even bat an eye?" Meghan jested, jabbing James squarely in the chest.

"Actually, no." James cleared his throat awkwardly. "I haven't taken anyone home with me in two years, not since Jessinta."

"You don't have to tell me about her if you don't want to." God knew that Meghan had enough secrets of her own that she wasn't telling him.

"There's not much to say," James still sounded bitter, even after all these years. "We dated on and off for five years and even contemplated moving in together, that was before I discovered that she had stolen my research paper, months of research and data that I had gathered on the prevalence of infant mortality in the outback, gone. She published it under her name, and as I hadn't informed anyone of my research, there was no peer proof that it was mine," he shook his head, still furious at the way that Jessinta had tried to justify her actions, how she claimed that it had been done for both of them, that she knew that he would never publish it himself. He still found himself wondering how he could have maintained a relationship with her for so long.

"I'm sorry," Meghan's genuine concern showed on her face, and he leant across, kissing her softly, wondering at how she was able to keep her compassion when she lived and worked in such an isolating, unforgiving environment.

"Anyway," James clapped his hands together, changing the subject abruptly. "Mother has been busy getting everything ready for you, she is putting you up in one of the guest cottages they have, Star." Seeing the flash of disappointment dancing across her eyes, James hastened to explain "Her first choice would have been to have you in the main house with everyone else, but as she was quick to tell me, I didn't let her know early enough that we would be joining them this year, and she has already commandeered one of the bedrooms in the main house to use as a storage space."

"It sounds lovely," she blushes a deep red, trying to keep the hint of disappointment out of her voice.

"You are so cute when you try to placate someone, but I am afraid your blush gives you away every time," he pushes a strand of hair away from her face. "What is it that you are not telling me?"

"I was hoping to stay in the Ivy cottage," she admitted, "it looks romantic," she finishes a bit guiltily, realising once the words have left her lips that there is nothing romantic about their relationship, that it was based entirely on mutual lust and desire, and nothing else.

James smiled and drew her close, melding her body to fit his so perfectly that she could feel the heat of his arousal through his jeans, watching her pupils dilate with lust. "Did I tell you that I am staying in the Blaze cottage?" James whispered into Meghan's ear, trailing a line of kisses down her throat. "Right next door to you in the Star cottage, our own little hideaway, far away from the main house that will be full of my sisters and their families, the blessing of a late decision," he cupped her breast through the cotton fabric of her dress, thumbing her nipple until he felt it pucker beneath his touch.

"James!" Meghan's voice was thick with need. "We can't."

"We can," he silenced her protest with his mouth, giving her nipple a quick twist between his thumb and forefinger, causing her to cry out in surprise. "We are in the middle of nowhere Meg, no one else is around for miles. I need to feel you wrapped around me, I need to bury myself deep inside your core, I have been far too long without you." On some level, James knew that he should be worried. He had been apart from Meghan for less than twenty-four hours and was feeling unsettled by the lack of physical contact, something that he was not used to, something that had never bothered him in his past relationships. Standing, he pulled Meghan to her feet, slowly lifting her dress up over her head, discarding it on the blanket next to them. Standing before him, wearing a plunging emerald green lace bra that barely contained her breasts, and a matching lace thong, he thought he had never seen anything so breathtakingly stunning.

He smiled down at her look of concentration as her slender fingers made quick work of the buttons on his shirt, impatiently pushing it off his chest to splay her hands over his chest, sighing in delight as she bent to kiss his muscled chest, slowly working her way down his chest towards the waistband of his pants, deftly undoing his button fly, placing a kiss on the bulge straining to be free, pushing his pants down for him to kick them off. James returned the favour, removing her bra, enjoying the sight of her breasts puckering under his gaze, dropping to his knees, biting her panties between his teeth and teasing them down her legs. James watched with undisguised lust as Meghan laid back against the picnic blanket and lazily let her legs fall open, never breaking eye contact, giving him a perfect view of her silky folds waiting for him. Manoeuvring to kneel between her legs, James wasted no time with formalities, grabbing her hips and pulling her closer, using the head of his throbbing length to tease her sensitive nub, enjoying watching her hips buck beneath him in an attempt to get closer to him, to draw him inside.

Laughing with the delight of rediscovering each other, James slid painstakingly slowly into Meghan's soft centre, savouring the moans he elicited from her, loving the way his name sounded on her lips. He slowly built up a steady rhythm, matched thrust for thrust by Meghan, her skin burning with desire, frantic with need. With a final thrust, James tipped them over the abyss, his triumphant shout mingling with Meghan's fevered calling of his name. Collapsing in each other's arms, they lay, totally spent, on the picnic blanket until the shade shifted, allowing the heat of the sun to bear down on top of them. Neither wanting to risk sunburn in sensitive places, they reluctantly dressed, making themselves presentable once again for the rest of the journey. Back on the road, Meghan was pensive, she was starting to think that agreeing to James's no strings attached relationship had been a mistake, a very big mistake and she wondered if she would be brave enough to walk away when the time came. The closer they drew to James's parent's property, the more Meghan wished she could change her mind and turn back. Looking across at James, singing off-key to Alicia Keyes, she had a sinking feeling that it was already far too late.

CHAPTER EIGHT

As they drove through the cattle gate, dust billowed up behind the car, blocking the view of the main road. No turning back now, Meghan thought grimly to herself. Pulling up at the impressive stone house, Meghan found her door being opened before she was engulfed in a wave of people, a sea of hugs and kind words, and motherly kisses on her cheek. To her horror Meghan found herself tearing up, relieved when James broke through the throng of his relatives and slung his arm around her neck, tucking her into his side.

"Enough Dad! Mum! It has been a long drive, one that Meghan started with a migraine. I'm going to take her down to the cottages to unpack." James waved away his sister's light-hearted banter and suggestions on how they should unpack, feeling slightly sorry when he saw his mother's hurt look. It had been too long since he had been home. "We'll come up to the house in half an hour, we can catch up then." James kissed his mother on the cheek, pulled their suitcases from the trunk of the car, and led Meghan off in the direction of the cottages.

"Are you okay?" James asked once they were out of earshot of his family, not having missed her watery eyes or ramrod straightening of her spine when his mother had hugged her.

"I'm fine." James let it go until he had opened the door of the Star cottage for her, putting his suitcase down in the sitting area next to hers, before giving her a quick tour of the cottage, deliberately pointing out the private courtyard secluded from view, earning him a small smile from Meghan. He pulled her swiftly down onto the outdoor lounger, holding her tightly on his lap.

"Tell me what happened back there?"

"Your mum hugged me." Meghan sounded incredulous at the thought.

"Yes, she's always been a hugger." James smiled at the memory. "I can tell her to stop if you would like me to?" James meant it, even if it would mean hurting his mother's feelings, something he had never done for anyone else. James squirmed, uncomfortable knowing that had Jessinta ever mentioned not wanting to be hugged, James would have told her to endure it for the short time they were here. Meghan was different. Complicated. Ever so dangerous.

"God, no!" Meghan sounded horrified at the thought. "It's just that when she hugged me, she *really* hugged me, you know?" James did. "I miss my mum," Meghan whispered so softly James wasn't sure he had actually heard her.

"Meg, I'm sorry. It was selfish of me to bring you here; I should have thought about you more, and what it would mean for you, coming home with me. It's just that I thought it would be fun, and less complicated if the entire hospital doesn't see us getting involved," James admitted. So that was it, Meghan thought, ice running through her veins. He wants to keep his no strings attached relationship separate from his career. Well, she could understand that, it will certainly be better for her if the whole hospital isn't gossiping about her. Although not a sackable offence, if anyone else at work knew, she would certainly be subjected to some pretty snarky comments from their colleagues, especially once their crazy little affair had fizzled out.

"I hate lying to her." Meghan finally spoke. "It isn't right, not when she is so happy for you. Promise me something," she turned suddenly, the intensity in her eyes causing James's breath to catch in his throat.

"Anything," he spoke without thinking and could have kicked himself for it.

"When we get back to Alice Springs, you call your parents and tell them that I broke up with you, that it was my decision. I don't want them thinking you are incapable of committing." Interesting that she cared what his parents thought of him, and would happily take the blame, even though they both knew James had set all the rules from the start, a realisation that was starting to sit very uneasily with him now.

"Meg-" he started.

"I'm going to get changed before we go to the house." Meghan cut him off and strode inside, grateful for some distance between them.

"Your house is gorgeous Mrs-"

"Don't you dare! Everyone calls me Zonja," arms linked together, Meghan was being given the grand tour of the main house, and Zonja was delighted to have someone new to show around. "And this," she gestured theatrically, "is our favourite room." Meghan felt her mouth gape open as she looked around in awe. The room in question was a large luscious grassed indoor courtyard, so cool and inviting, Meghan knew that if she was living here, it would be her favourite room too. Surrounded on all four sides, the courtyard backed onto the entertainment area, the open plan kitchen, the library, and the master bedroom. Set up in the middle of the courtyard was a large plank table laden with cakes, sandwiches, and sugar cookies; jugs of drinks and glasses of flowers strewn throughout. Meghan smiled weakly, feeling rather like a fraud, and crossed to sit next to James.

"So, how did you meet our boy, Meghan?" Gerhardus was striking, and Meghan found herself wondering if James would look like that when he was older.

"We work together dad, I told you this," James answered for her, quick to nip that line of questioning in the bud.

"What? She can't answer for herself?" Gerhardus insisted.

"Meghan?" James, smiling, gestured for her to answer his dad.

"We work together," Meghan parroted, catching James's eye and sharing a chuckle. "I work on the children's ward Gerhardus, James and I actually met at the scene of an accident, a case of the right place at the right time for the driver."

Gerhardus nodded approvingly. "I thought you must have known each other for a while, it shows with people, doesn't it?" Meghan, stealing a glance at James from the corner of her eye, agreed that it did indeed. Leaning back in his chair, James draped his arm over the back of

Meghan's chair, his fingers toying with the ends of the stray tendrils of her hair that had wriggled loose.

The scent of her perfume caught on the wind and wafted around him, enveloping him in the heady aroma of jasmine, lemon and honeysuckle. He breathed deeply, committing it to memory, letting it wash over him and settle on his skin. Laughing deeply at the story Meghan was regaling his mother with, James felt eyes on him and looked up to see his father studying him studiously with troubled eyes. James glanced away, unable to hold his father's gaze, and swallowed guiltily. Sensing his discomfort, Meghan reached for his hand, lacing her fingers with his and giving it a squeeze which he returned. James could understand why his parents were concerned, but seriously, Meghan was *not* Jessinta, a fact James was becoming all too aware of. He was beginning to think that bringing Meghan here was a mistake, he was no longer so sure of himself. Could he say goodbye to her in a few short weeks? Would he? Suddenly feeling as if he was being suffocated, James stands abruptly, drops a kiss on Meghan's cheek, and goes out to play with his nieces and nephews.

As the sun slowly started to set on the horizon, Meghan sat at the edge of the pool with Zonja, feet paddling in the cool water. The afternoon had turned hot, and the family had moved out to the patio. While the kids had made a beeline for the waterslide, the adults had tossed some salads and started a barbeque for dinner. The smells wafting down from the patio were delicious and Meghan was embarrassed when her stomach gave a low rumble, but Zonja just brushed it off, she liked to see girls with healthy appetites. Whether the warm country air, the long drive or the delicious food she ate, an exhausted Meghan was happy to excuse herself shortly after dessert, the feeling of another headache starting to form. Although planning a long soak in the deep bathtub, the double bed in her cottage looked so inviting that Meghan laid straight down instead, intending to get up and run her bath once her head had stopped pounding. Stopping off on his way to his cottage,

James found her sound asleep, covering her gently with the blanket and leaving her.

CHAPTER NINE

By the time James wandered up to the house, breakfast was already well and truly underway. Greeted with a chorus of good mornings, he was surprised to see that he had actually slept in, something he never usually does. Pouring himself a coffee, he leant back on the kitchen bench, watching Meghan nurse Harry, his chubby fingers full of drool, gurgling up at her. James had told her that his nieces and nephews ranged in age from two months old up to almost ten years old, all as rambunctious and as noisy as each other, and all very much adored additions to their families. There were so many new faces and happy children vying for attention that Meghan knew she would never get everyone's names right. Meghan knew that Elspeth and her husband Daniel had Micah and Joe before their daughter Charley came along five years later; Fleur and Richard's family was complete with Gabby, Ella and Annie; and that Lusea and Mark didn't know if they would have another baby or not, even though they already had Hunter, Jerry, Samuel, Georgina, Emma and Piper.

It was James's eldest sister, Arabella, that Meghan instantly connected with. Arabella and her husband Rob had been desperate for a child and had tried anything over the years, she confessed to Meghan, even fertility statues. Unsuccessful, they had made peace with the fact they wouldn't become parents and had instead devoted themselves to being the best aunt and uncle they could be. Shortly after her forty-fourth birthday Arabella had been ill, and unable to shake it after a few months, had finally gone to James, convinced something was seriously wrong. James had listened to her symptoms, taken a blood test to confirm his diagnosis, and told her to call Rob, they were finally expecting. Baby Harry was now a chubby two-month-old, and the apple of everyone's eye. A content baby, happy to be passed from one set of loving arms to another, with no shortage of adoring relatives to coo and fuss over him. Even the other children doted on him, smattering his face with kisses and constantly running back to check if he was okay.

Meghan smiled down at Harry, a baby in this family was very much celebrated and treasured, unlike she was, her smile faltered slightly. She held him close, breathing in his baby scent, her heart squeezing tightly in her chest. She knew it would hurt, she knew she shouldn't be holding him, this perfect little baby, shouldn't be opening herself up to more anguish and despair, but she couldn't help it. Meghan looked down at Harry, blowing spit raspberries at her, and bent her head, placing a soft kiss on his downy head, squeezing her eyes shut tight, imagining just for a moment, that things were different, wondering what it would be like if this were her baby. James watched her face, his smile slipping as he saw her stricken expression, a solitary tear sliding down her face before she brushed it away unnoticed by anyone else. James watched as Meghan reluctantly handed Harry back to Arabella, didn't miss the slight shake in her hands, or the way she tried not to follow him with her eyes. Downing his coffee, he crossed the room with firm strides, taking Meghan's hand and pulling her into a strong embrace. "I missed you last night, are you feeling better today?"

"I'm sorry, I just haven't been able to shake these headaches." Meghan reached up to kiss James's cheek, aware of the small eyes in the room. "I'm sure I'll be fine in a day or two."

James stared intently into her eyes, sensing there was more than she was telling him. "If you have finished breakfast maybe we can steal away for an hour? I'll show you my secret hiding spot," he whispered in her ear, suddenly keen to share it with her.

"I'd like that," she gave him a small smile.

Promising to be back in time for a game of cricket before lunch, James took Meghan's hand and led her down the back steps and across the fenced yard, over to the double-storey barn. They stepped inside and waited, blinking furiously until their eyes adjusted to the dimness of the light. "When I was a small boy, tired of my sister's silly games, I used to sneak out here and climb up there," James tugged on the ladder leading to the hay loft. "Shall we?" He held out his hand for Meghan, helping her up before climbing up after her. "I would stay here for hours, reading, until mum would call us in for dinner. She always pretended to be so shocked when I came in covered in dust and hay, but I think she knew," James laughed at the memory, he had loved growing up on the property, surrounded by open spaces to explore, and cattle to boss around.

"You had a happy childhood, didn't you?" Meghan asked, a wistful tone to her voice.

"The best! What about you Meg? What happened when you were holding Harry to make you look so sad?" James reached for her hand, stung when she brushed him off, choosing to cross her arms over her middle instead.

"You are very close with your sisters," Meghan knew it sounded like an accusation. "It is pretty obvious, even though you say they are a force to be reckoned with, just how much you love them. I've been watching you play with your nieces and nephews, James, you are so good with them, it is obvious that you are a pretty fun uncle," Meghan could feel her voice starting to break. She would not cry over this, not in front of James, she scolded herself mentally. "I know that you must have been deeply hurt when Jessinta betrayed you, but why are you still single? Why haven't you gone out there and found a Mrs Cristo? Don't you want to get married someday and have a family of your own?"

James watched Meghan's face as she spoke. He had a sinking feeling that hers was a trick question, that he was somehow being baited into a trap that he was unable to recognise.

He shrugged as he answered her. "I always thought that I would get married, yes, and it was something that I certainly thought a lot about when I was younger, before choosing to go to medical school," he answered truthfully.

"And now?" she prompted, barely breathing, desperately keen to hear his answer.

He gave her a long hard look, never breaking eye contact, contemplating his answer carefully. "Yes, in theory, I would still like to get married and, hopefully, have children." Eight, nine, ten…Meghan opened her eyes to find James still staring at her, his intense brown eyes boring into her soul. She swallowed thickly.

"Phew, lucky for us then that this is just physical," she chirped, determined to make light of things, "we are complete opposites, we would never work out as a couple!" She forced herself to smile at James, a little too brightly, ignoring the look of disbelief, or was it sadness, that skipped through his eyes. No, she must be imagining it, she means nothing to James outside of a bit of physical fun during the rest of his tenure in Alice Springs, and she would do well to remember that.

"Why do you keep doing that?" James furrowed his brow in consternation. "You ask me a question, having already made up your mind about the situation before I even answer. Then when I do answer, you act like it is of no consequence and brush it off with a joke."

"I don't do that," Meghan rebutted, half-heartedly.

"Yes, Meg, you do," although firm, his voice was still gentle, as if he were explaining something to a small child. "Ever since the first time I kissed you, you have been trying to push me away, keeping me at arm's length. At first, I thought you were genuinely uninterested in me," he flashed her his trademark sexy smile, "but I soon discovered that that was not the issue. When you agreed to my no strings attached suggestion, I was thrilled with the prospect of being able to get to discover you, all of you, without any expectations or relationship conventions hindering me, but Meg, every time the status of our relationship is brought up, you get defensive and start to put distance between you and me, did you think I hadn't noticed? Now, you asked me the other night if I had changed my mind about our relationship, if I wanted it to be less than casual, I wonder though Meg, if I should be asking you the same thing?"

"Yeah, right," Meghan scoffed. "As if! Are you really that egotistical that you think I would find you so irresistible that I would allow myself to, what? Fall in love with you? Seriously, James, is that what you are suggesting? Get a grip!"

"Then what is it, Meg? A general annoyance that I want to get married and have kids or is it that I want to get married and have kids, and you don't figure into those plans?" As soon as the words were out, he wished he could have taken them back, Meghan's face lose all semblance of colour. He winced with the knowledge that he had been cruel to say those things to her, and James was never deliberately cruel.

"I can't believe that you just said that," Meghan hissed. "As it happens, Mr I Know Everything, I have no intentions of ever marrying, or of ever having any children," Meghan infused her words with a tone of disgust, forcing herself to shudder at the statement as if the very idea was repulsive to her. "Could you imagine it?!" Meghan could, and had, many, many times, which was the real problem. Oh, if only he knew, her heart cried out, if only he knew he wouldn't be so smug with her, so quick to be so self-righteous.

James watched her with disbelief. Something didn't add up, this Meghan was not the Meghan that he knew, it was as if she was deliberately trying to hide something from him, and he didn't like it one bit.

"Well," Meghan stood up, brushing the loose hay off her bottom, "your mum said I could wander down to the creek behind the house if I promised to be back before it gets too hot," Meghan felt as if her face must surely be cracking from all the forced smiling she was doing. "If you don't mind, I will go and have a look at it now," before she had finished speaking, Meghan had already started down the loft ladder.

"If you would like to, feel free." James's tone was clipped, and Meghan tried not to let it affect her. "I would offer to accompany you, but under the circumstances perhaps it is best if you go alone. Besides, I promised my nieces and nephews that I would play cricket with them, and I would hate for you to have to spend any more time than was absolutely necessary with them, seeing as how you detest children so much. I guess I will see you back at the house for lunch?" Meghan nodded at him, opened her mouth to say something, then changed her mind and closed it again, and walked off in the direction of the creek. James watched her go with a sinking feeling in his stomach that he wasn't quite ready to name yet.

Meghan took the well-worn path from the house to the creek, grass worn down to dirt over the years, and tried to imagine James as a father. He would be kind and compassionate, with rules to keep everyone safe. He would be firm when he needed to be, she decided, even though he wouldn't like it. He would treat playtime as a sacred honour and keep secrets and confidences. "Stop it!" she hissed to herself. What had happened to her? How had she let him of all people, past her defences? She had made such a colossal mistake, she should never have agreed to any type of fling with him, no matter how logical it had sounded at the time. She should have known. "Stupid, stupid, stupid!" she fumed. And where had it gotten her? Stuck in the middle of nowhere with a man she couldn't keep her hands off, a man who thought she was beautiful and precious, a man she could never really have. It was the cruellest punishment, she decided, seeing what you could have, if only things were different, all the while knowing that you will never have it. Meghan stopped suddenly and looked around. Where was the creek? She was sure Zonja had said it was just behind the house. Meghan turned in a slow circle, brow furrowed, unable to see anything except grass and trees. Where was the house? She hadn't walked that far, surely?

"Where the hell is she?" James spat out, slamming his hand down on the table, ignoring the way it shook.

"James," his mother cautioned, motioning to the children sitting around the table.

"I'll be damned if I am going to sit around here and wait any longer. I'm going to find her," he stood, crammed his hat back down on his head, and strode towards the front door, stomach churning with fear.

"James, wait," his dad called out, easily catching up to him on the front veranda. "We just want you to be careful," he gestured towards James's mum, hovering at the front door. "We haven't seen you this happy since...Well, in a long time. Whatever happened between you and Meghan, don't be too rash to react."

James stared at him incredulously. "You think I am the reason she wandered off?" Did his parents really have that much of a lack of faith in him? Seriously! "Well dad, you may be right, but not in the way you think," James pressed his lips into a long hard line, thinking. "Do you want to know the truth dad? I mean, the real truth?" James swallowed hard and watched his parents exchange a worried glance. "Meghan and I are not in a relationship, we haven't even dated, this thing between us is purely physical," he ignored his mother's shocked gasp and continued on "and, as she is so very keen to keep reminding me, she likes it that way," James didn't even bother to hide the bitterness in his voice. "Newsflash dad, even if I wanted more, and I am not saying that I do, she doesn't!" And with that James turned on his heel and headed for the creek, where he only hoped that he wouldn't find Meghan's injured or drowned body. Then again, he thought wryly, maybe that wouldn't be so bad, at least then it wouldn't be his fault, not entirely anyway.

CHAPTER TEN

Mortified at the thought of someone needing to come out and look for her like a silly lost child, Meghan decided instead to try and find her way back to the house, but as the minutes turned into hours and darkness began to fall, she had to finally admit the truth, she was well and truly lost. Sinking into the ochre dirt at the base of a small grove of trees, Meghan looked around apprehensively. When she had started out for the creek James didn't mention needing to watch out for snakes or lizards or spiders, but then again, why would he? He thought she was going to take a quick walk to the creek and back, not wander off to goodness knows where. What if she isn't even on their property anymore? Meghan didn't think it was likely, but who knew where the property lines were on a cattle station? It wasn't as if they had standard fencing as they did in suburban Alice Springs. And what about the cattle! Meghan's head flew in all directions, trying to ascertain if there were any roaming nearby. Were they in pens or paddocks or whatever cattle stayed in? What a fine mess she had managed to get herself into now.

An uneasiness settled around Meghan, what if James wasn't even looking for her? What if he didn't even know she was missing? For all she knew he would just assume that she was still mad and had gone straight to bed. "He wouldn't though, would he?" she asked the darkness. In the silence that answered her, Meghan had to concede that it was, in fact, entirely possible. He was obviously mad with her, she had deliberately set out to hurt him with her callous comments on motherhood, trying to get a rise out of him. He had been right, though, about her. She had used every possible reason to point out to him that she was not in this for the long haul, reminding him again and again of their agreement. She was only grateful for the fact that he didn't know why, he thought that she had been acting out of a sense of selfishness, but he couldn't be more wrong. Meghan was acting out of a sense of self-preservation, she knew that making James hate her was the only way to ensure that something long-term would not eventuate, saving herself a lot of heartache in the process. So why then did it hurt so much to do?

Not having any luck locating Meghan at the creek, James had circled back to the house and collected a backpack, throwing in items he knew he might need; a satellite phone, some bottled water, a two-way radio, a basic first aid kit, a space blanket, and some non-perishable food items. He collected a heavy-duty torch, mapped out where he thought Meghan might have gotten lost, a secondary path that merged with the path to the creek, and promised to check in every thirty minutes with the house via his radio. James knew the worry evident in his family member's faces was reflected on his own, their concern for him, and for Meghan, demonstrated in the way they volunteered to head out to look with him, an offer James declined. They had no idea where she would be, or what state she would be in when they found her, and there was no point in anyone else getting turned around in the dark. He would search alone, his family would coordinate the search, carefully checking off the areas on the map as James searched them, that way he wouldn't be searching aimlessly. It was agreed that if he hadn't found her by midnight, they would alert the local police, as that would make it over twelve hours since she had last been seen, and they all knew what danger could transpire in twelve hours. James tried to push the thought aside as he headed out into the dark, carrying the thermos of coffee his mother had thrust into his hands at the last minute, but no matter how hard he tried, visions of Meghan injured or unconscious kept running through his head, and he quickened his pace.

Melting, that's what she was. Meghan had no idea how it could be so unimaginably hot in the middle of the night, but it was. "I will never again complain about the heat in Alice Springs," she stated aloud to the darkness. She was sorely tempted to take her dress off, but the thought of sitting in her underwear in the dirt didn't much appeal to her, without any light to see with, she had no way of knowing if there were ants or bugs scuttling around, or worse, lizards! She shuddered at the thought. Oh, how she hated lizards, with their pulsing little bodies, their sticky, webbed feet, those beady little eyes and the way they scurried everywhere. They freaked her out, even though she knew, logically, that she was hundreds of times their size, they still gave her the heebee jeebees. Disconcerted and unable to stand the silence any longer, Meghan took a deep breath and started to sing.

James stopped and pulled out his map, marking off another square. His watch confirmed what he already knew, he had another forty minutes until the police would be called. Where was she? James had been out searching now for almost seven hours, methodically searching back and forth, determined not to overlook anything. He had taken the secondary path leading away from the creek, towards the endless expanse of land they used to graze cattle, he had checked, with his heart in his mouth, the edges of the dams for skid marks or tracks, and still, there was no sign of her. How far could she have wandered? He looked around, the moonlight casting an eerie glow over the land. There were a few scraggly trees scattered ahead, he would search there before radioing home and giving his family the little information he had. Stuffing his map back in his backpack, James hesitated, ears picking up. What was that noise? It sounded like...someone in pain! Fear gripped him and he plunged through the darkness, following the sound as best he could, emerging beside a cluster of gum trees, the sound coming to an abrupt halt.

"Good grief, now I'm seeing things," Meghan cackled hysterically, unable to stop her hysterical laughing at the sight of James.

"Meg? Oh my God! Are you okay?" James crossed the clearing and knelt next to her, shining his torch on her, looking for injuries.

"Are you real?" Meghan asked incredulously, poking James's chest with her finger.

"Yes." James snapped, brushing her hand away. "Now, where are you hurt?"

"I'm not hurt." Meghan sniffed indignantly. Here she was, thinking that he wouldn't be looking for her, but he did, even if it seemed as if he would have rather be doing something, anything, else.

"What? But I heard you screaming." James paused in his search to look at her, taking in the way her chin was thrust out stubbornly, the way her eyes were full of unshed tears. Hell!

"I was singing a popular rock song if you must know, geez!" she crossed her arms over her chest, glaring at him. James gaped at her, mouth hanging open, before breaking into a smile.

"Meg," he cupped her face tenderly in his hands. "Are you all right?"

"No," Meghan croaked, lip wobbling. "I'm incredibly hot, tired, filthy dirty and probably surrounded by a colony of lizards at this moment, not to-" she was cut off midsentence as James's mouth claimed hers in a searing kiss, so full of longing and promise, it brought Meghan to tears.

"Meg, don't cry, it's okay." James produced a bottle of water from his backpack and passed it to Meghan, who unscrewed it with shaky hands and took a huge gulp.

"It's not okay, not when you kiss me like that. You can't," Meghan sucked in a fortifying breath, "kiss me anymore, James, you can't. I can't do it, this thing, us, I just can't do it anymore," she ended on a hiccup, large blue eyes looking at him through wet lashes, horrified at her outburst. She hadn't meant to say anything, had determined not to utter a word to him until after they were back in Alice Springs, confident that she would be able to avoid him for the remainder of their trip. Anything to stop arousing his suspicions.

"I can't believe you," James pushed himself up from the ground and paced around the small clearing. "Might I remind you, Meghan, that you agreed to this no strings attached relationship, you went into this willingly. If you want out, fine, I won't force you Meghan, not even I am that desperate!" His barb hit her exactly where he had intended it to, all emotion sapped from her, replaced with a cold dread spreading throughout her body, emanating from her chest and seeping down to her toes. Fine, she lifted her chin, determined not to show him how much his words had hurt her. For someone who had just gotten what it was they wanted, Meghan felt decidedly bereft.

He snatched up the backpack and withdrew the two-way radio, stepping away from Meghan and calling home to let them know that he had found her and that they would be heading back shortly, his family's relief coming across the radio loud and clear. He gave Meghan a withering look, ignoring how the remnants of her earlier tears affected him. "Do you think you can walk?" He asked sarcastically. "Or should I carry you?" Meghan stood up slowly, not even bothering to answer him, feeling her heart break a little more inside as he turned away from her and strode off, expecting her to follow obediently behind him. She thought of refusing to go with him, but what good would that serve? He would most likely just throw her over his shoulder like a naughty child and carry her back to the house. Or worse yet, leave her here as if she was of no consequence. Even in daylight, she knew that she would never be able to find her way back to the house on her own. Already he was a long way in front of her and she had to scramble to catch up, not keen on experiencing his ire anymore tonight.

Stumbling around in the pitch-black bush armed with only a torch and a sliver of moon was not the best idea that he had ever had, James admitted to himself. He could hear Meghan stumbling around behind him, trying valiantly to keep up with his fast pace fuelled by anger, but callously refused to slow down for her. He knew he had been an idiot, was still acting like an idiot, but was too angry to care. Hearing Meghan gasp, and the unmistakable sound of something hitting the ground, he ground out a curse and turned back. What the hell was wrong with him? Why was he acting like such a jerk? He was the one who originally told Meghan he was only interested in a no-strings relationship, nothing serious and certainly nothing long-term. So why was he now acting all bent out of shape, like a boyfriend who had just been dumped? The thought shocked him, was that how he had started to see them, their relationship? As something more permanent? Meghan had scrabbled back to her feet and joined him, not looking him in the eyes, instead brushing straight past him, ignoring the ache in her ankle that now matched the one in her heart.

"Meghan, stop, you're limping," the command in his voice made James wince and he reached out his hand and caught her by the elbow, guiding her to a nearby fallen tree to sit on.

"I'm fine, James," Meghan huffed, exhaling a pent-up breath. She crossed her arms over her chest and continued, "there is no need for you to have to worry, I am sure I can make it back to the house."

"What happened?" Looking down at her James knew he had to ask.

"I tripped over something okay, no big deal," Meghan sniped.

"I'm not talking about your ankle," James squatted in front of her, "I'm talking about us, Meg. I don't understand. Yesterday we were fine, at least I thought we were."

"Oh." Meghan refused to meet his gaze, instead staring intently down at her shoes. "It was only ever a casual fling James, you know that. As good as it has been, it is time to get back to reality," she looked at him defiantly, meeting and holding his gaze. "I am no longer interested in having a fling with you."

"Is that it, Meg? That's what you are going to say? Do you really expect me to believe that?" He raised an eyebrow at her. "I'll tell you what I think, I think that agreeing to come here with me was the easy part, I think that now that you are here, surrounded by family, you are starting to feel differently. I think that this thing between us has started to feel less like the no strings attached casual fling it started out as being and has instead started to feel very much like the real thing, and you don't like that. I think you enjoy having your perfect ordered world the way it was before you took a chance, you enjoy being in control and shutting everyone out, I think you quite enjoy being alone." James refused to drop her gaze. "Tell me I'm wrong," he challenged.

CHAPTER ELEVEN

"You can talk," Meghan fired up. "Claiming you want a no strings attached casual fling because you are focused on your career. Ha! Hung up on your ex, Jessinta, is more accurate. So how does it work James? She spurned you and so now you are going to just stay unattached, emotionally at least, until you die? For what purpose? To spite her? To stop yourself from getting hurt again? You are such a hypocrite, lecturing me about being alone when you are doing the same thing, worse even, for you, because although you claim to want this no strings attached casual fling with me, you also expect to get married and have kids someday," Meghan was well and truly screaming now, not bothering to be at all quiet in her anger. "How supremely lucky for you that I happen to be here, filling a gap, until you find this perfect woman to marry and reproduce with," she finished bitterly.

"Jealous Meg?" James asked quietly, dangerously close to Meghan's ear. "For all you talk about keeping things casual, you seem pretty interested in what I want in the future. Perhaps I was wrong about you, maybe you have designs on being the future Mrs Cristo, is that it Meg? Is that why you are happy to bide your time in the children's ward? Are you husband-hunting, hoping to snare a doctor and the prestigious title of being a doctor's wife?"

"Go to hell!" Meghan spat, shoving him away from her, stomping off as he fell onto his back on the ground.

"Not so fast," scrambling up from the ground, James jogged over to Meghan, grabbing her by the elbow and turning her to face him. There was a dangerous glint in his eyes that sent shivers down Meghan's spine, and she was unable to look away. "I'm not letting you out of my sight until we are back at the house, we don't want you getting lost in the bush again, do we?"

"I'm not a complete imbecile," Meghan glared at James, "I was perfectly happy waiting out here until morning when I could have walked back home by myself, you didn't have to come out looking for me, especially since it has so obviously been a hardship for you."

"So that's what you think, is it?" James scowled down at her. "Just what do you suppose I have been doing all afternoon while you have been sulking out here? Honestly! You are so infuriating!" He turned away from Meghan and paced back and forth. "As it happens, I have been out of my mind with worry, searching every place I could think of for you to be. Do you have any idea how it felt, Meg, to have to search the edge of the creek for you? Expecting to find your unconscious or mangled body?" James, having given up any semblance of politeness, was now shouting at the top of his voice, arms moving animatedly as he spoke. "While you have been sitting out here, apparently convincing yourself of my indifference towards you, towards us, towards this situation of ours, our relationship, or whatever you want to call it, I have been out of my mind with worry. Darn it, Meg, I could throttle you!"

James glared at Meghan. He expected her to feel bad, remorseful even, but what he hadn't been expecting was her to burst into tears and sink to her knees on the ground, sobs wracking her body. Meghan was mortified. It was one thing to act angry towards James when he was giving her the silent treatment, it was quite another thing to actually hear him tell her he had been worried. About her. Covering her face with her hands, Meghan tried to regain her composure, gasping for breath in between sobs.

"Meg, I'm sorry." James kneeled beside her and pulled her into his arms. "I was acting like a prize jerk. I was just so worried about you, and now," he shrugged his shoulders, "I guess I am just confused. I thought we were having fun, and I am so sorry Meg, if I did anything to upset you," he kissed the top of her head and held her until her sobs subsided.

"Believe me, it is not you, it is me, all me. James, I'm sorry. I thought you would be too mad at me to come and find me, and then I was so relieved that you had come for me, but you were so mad!" She hiccupped. "James," Meghan looked into his face, the moonlight illuminating his features, and cupped his face, kissing him softly on the lips, "you were right before, I wasn't telling you the whole truth, but I'd like to."

James sat up straight and waited for Meghan to start speaking again, his eyes following her as she paced in front of him, hands wringing together. "You know I told you my parents have passed away," Meghan looked at James, who nodded his confirmation. "I was adopted when I was two years old. My biological mother was a drug addict, and when I was six months old, she left me alone in my crib while she went out to get high. By the time the neighbours tired of my crying and called the police, I was so dehydrated the only vein they could find for a drip was one in my ankle. I spent months in hospital before I was placed with my foster parents, who were later granted permission to adopt me. They couldn't have loved me more if I was biologically theirs," Meghan smiled at the memory, a faraway look in her eyes. "We didn't have much in the way of money, but I wanted for nothing, James." Sighing deeply, Meghan turned to face him, knowing that she owed him this, he needed to hear the truth. "About five years ago I met someone, a young surgical registrar at the hospital where I worked. Michael was charming," Meghan grimaced at the memory of just how charming he had been, "and convinced me to go out with him. He was very...persuasive about certain things." Meghan had started to wring her hands together again, and James grew cold, knowing what was coming. "He was my first, and too selfish to care about anything other than himself, which led to it being traumatic for me," Meghan shrugged and looked at James in the eyes. "There hasn't been anyone else since Michael. Until you," she confessed quietly, causing James to grow uncomfortably hard with the thought.

"He pursued me relentlessly, and within a few weeks, we were engaged. Michael seemed to feel that a large society wedding was expected of his family and despite my reservations, he started to make the preparations. It wasn't until we discussed the issue of children during our pre-wedding counselling with the church minister that things started to go bad. You see, Michael hadn't realised I was adopted, it had never come up and I naively didn't think it was even an issue. Michael disagreed. He told me in no uncertain terms that he would not be allowed to marry a girl with no bloodlines," Meghan's voice faltered. "His parents wouldn't allow such a union. As the only son in the family, Michael was expected to eventually precede his father at his family medical centre, and Michael would expect a son to follow in his footsteps. He wasn't interested in taking a gamble on faulty stock, and as he told me, I have no background, meaning that I could be anybody. If he married me, there was no telling what sort of children the union would produce and raised with the knowledge that he deserves the best, Michael wouldn't risk it. He wouldn't be able to maintain his image if any children born were damaged." Meghan would never forget the day that Michael had told her that, the day she finally grew up and stopped believing in fairy tales.

"It was a deal-breaker for him." Meghan continued in a small voice unrecognisable from her own. "As if I wouldn't have loved and wanted any children born to me, it was all I ever wanted, before him." She sighed deeply. "He called the wedding off, something my parents were glad for. They had never liked him and seeing what he had done to me didn't do anything to change their opinion of him. A few months later he married the very rich daughter of a family friend and they have four kids now, all perfect carbon copies of him. So, you see James," Meghan sat back down next to James, ignoring the way her traitorous body responded to his proximity, "I don't *want* to be alone, I don't *want* to be lonely," her voice cracked, "but what choice have I? No man should have to gamble away his chance of having his dream of a family, especially not on someone like me." With deliberate slowness, James brought his mouth down on Meghan's, in a kiss so exquisitely sweet, that it brought tears to her eyes.

"Oh Meg, I am so sorry that happened to you, all of it." James cupped her face in his hands, tilting it upwards so he could see her properly. "I'll tell you this for certain, if two people are in love Meg, really in love, backgrounds aren't even mentioned, they aren't even considered. Real love is loving the person they are, not the background they came from. I don't know what will happen in the next few months, once my contract is up, I am not sure if I will remain in Alice Springs or move on to something different, but I do know this, I like you, Meg. I like spending time with you, you make me happy, and somewhere along the line, for me at least, it became more than just something physical. Yes, one day I would love to get married, and yes, one day, if the opportunity presented itself, I would love to have a family. I don't know what will happen Meg, but if you would only give us a chance, I would like to see where this relationship goes. Will you give us that chance Meg?" James held his breath, waiting, as an array of emotions swept across Meghan's face. She should say no, shouldn't she? She should say no and demand to be taken back to Alice Springs, yet, she trusted him, she knew, intrinsically, that James wouldn't hurt her, that he would do whatever he could to keep her from being hurt. Oh, how she ached to say yes, to have her heart open to the possibility of a maybe, to really experience what it would feel like to be James's girl, even if it was just for a short while.

"I can't James," Meghan choked out, "I want to, but I just can't risk it. You see, you say that it doesn't matter, you say that now, but I know, I know that in a year or two, maybe even five years, you will realise what you gave up and start to resent me. You might even try to talk me into having a baby, and I might even consider it, for you, but it would be a huge mistake! Do you want to know why I no longer work on maternity? Shortly after Michael left, I was on shift. A young couple came in, so young, and so in love. It was their first baby, they were so excited, they had all of the grandparents lined up outside, just waiting to hear that first cry," Meghan paused, tears streaming unbidden down her face. "Mum told me the reason they were both so excited was that they had both been in and out of the foster care system, they had never known a proper family until late childhood when they had been adopted by their respective families. Her labour was easy, what came after was the hardest day of my career. She had a beautiful baby girl, they named her Hope. She was born with a hereditary heart condition and passed away three hours later. If mum had known her medical history, she could have been screened better."

The walk back to the house was silent except for the snapping of sticks beneath their feet. Meghan didn't dare try to speak, she knew she had hurt James, and although that wasn't her intention, she was at a loss of words to explain how sorry she was and didn't trust her own emotions to try, the last thing she wanted was to shed more tears in front of him. James was too focused on his own thoughts to try speaking, an uneasy feeling had settled in the pit of his stomach, and he wasn't sure how to make everything better. Just the fact that he wanted to, spoke volumes to him about the strength of his own feelings, feelings that he had tried to pretend didn't exist. Perhaps he had been a fool to hide his true feelings from Meghan? Maybe if she knew how he really felt she would be more willing to take a chance on him, on them? James grudgingly admitted that it was probably too late, if he admitted his true feelings to her now, she was likely to think he was lying, trying to persuade her into giving them another chance. What a mess of things he had made! James had no idea how he was going to try to fix the situation he currently found himself in, only that he was, that he had to.

His family were all waiting for them on the front porch as James escorted Meghan through the gate, a grim look on his face and Meghan's streaked with tears, neither of which went unnoticed by those waiting for them. Although it was clear that James and Meghan had had a disagreement, he had no intention of elaborating for their audience. "See," he drawled contemptuously, "here she is safe and sound. After all, if there is one thing Meghan is good at, it is taking care of herself." Ignoring his mother's shocked admonishments and Meghan's embarrassed blush, James excused himself. "I need a drink," he stated dryly, heading into the house and through to the library where he poured himself a large brandy, swirling the liquid around in his glass, staring at it as if it held all the answers to the questions he sought.

"That was inexcusably rude," his father's stern voice invaded his scattered thoughts.

"Dad." James's voice held a warning, the last thing he needed was his dad meddling.

"No. I don't care what happened between you two out there, she is a guest in this home, and you will treat her with respect, is that understood?!"

James sat there, mouth hanging open, gaping at his father. His dad was actually telling him off, something that had not happened in years, although, to be fair, James conceded, his dad was right.

"You're right, Dad, I'll apologise before I go to bed tonight."

"For what?" His dad prompted him, raising his eyebrows in a questioning look.

"For being rude." James frowned. Hadn't his dad just told him off for that?

"And..." his dad left the word hanging in the air between them, a question, an invitation to share.

"And what Dad?"

"And for whatever else it was that you did." James's father held up his hands as a symbol of truce. "I know what you said, James, but I saw her face when you brought her back. She was distraught, people who are just in a relationship for the sex don't get distraught." James decided it was best not to question how his dad knew that, there were some things that James just did not want to know about his parents. "Whatever happened, you need to fix it. Unless..."

"Unless what?"

"Unless you don't love her, in which case you need to apologise respectfully and let her go. But if you do love her, and James, that is something that only you can decide for yourself, you need to decide if you can live without her, and if not, work out how to fix things between the two of you, before it is too late." His dad left him alone to think things through, telling him that Meghan was in the master bedroom with the ladies of the house, being pampered and cleaned up, but that as a doctor, maybe James would consider making sure that she didn't have any injuries that needed medical attention before he walked her back to her cottage. James got the message loud and clear. He sipped at his brandy slowly, drawing little comfort from the warm liquid. Could it be possible that he was in love with Meghan? His dad certainly seemed to think so, but it was impossible, wasn't it? They had only known each other for a few weeks, was that enough time to have fallen in love with someone? Before he had Meghan, James would have said an emphatic no, but now he wasn't so sure.

James thought back over the past few weeks, recalling details he wasn't even aware that he had stored away. He remembered how Meghan poked her tongue out of the corner of her mouth when she was concentrating hard enough on something, the way she used quotes from her favourite books in everyday conversations, and how her kindness towards others never changed, even though she was often scorned for it. She gave everything she had to others, without question, even though James knew that she was on a budget. Everything she did fascinated him, captivated him, and he realised with a jolt that he wanted to protect her, to keep her safe. Was it enough though? Was it love? James thought about his father's advice to let her go and tried to imagine it. What would it feel like, to walk away from Meghan? Cold dread seeped through James's body; his hands went clammy at the thought. He couldn't imagine it, he couldn't see himself without Meghan, and that told him everything that he needed to know. He had broken his own cardinal rule, he had gone ahead and fallen in love with her, and in the process, he had managed to belittle and humiliate her. He had done the very thing that he had accused her of, he had pushed her away, without even realising it.

As if in a daze, James walked through the house to the master bedroom, where he found Meghan brushing off his mother's concerns, assuring her that she was fine. He coughed to announce his presence, hating the way that Meghan's mouth thinned out and shutters came down over her eyes when she spied him standing in the doorway.

"Dad sent me to check on you, as a doctor," he had no idea why he was no longer able to form a coherent sentence. His mother shot him a look, clearly indicating that she thought he was an idiot, and for once, he was happy to agree.

"Fine," if Meghan's tone had been any cooler James would have been an ice sculpture. With his mother and sisters having strategically retreated from the room, James pulled out his blood pressure cuff and started taking his records. With Meghan checking out medically with nothing more than a mild case of heatstroke, James bid his family goodnight and stiffly walked Meghan to her cottage door, silently cursing himself every step of the way.

What was wrong with him? It was as if he could no longer even bear to look at her, now that he knew how he felt, he was terrified that she would be able to guess just from looking at his face. He stopped her in the doorway and took a steadying breath, cupping her face. "Meg, I am not giving up on you, or on us, after all, this land here has a certain magic in the air," he flashed her an uncertain smile, her eyes devoid of emotion. "Try and have a sleep-in tomorrow, I'll pop over and check in on you in the morning, call me if you need anything before then."

Reaching up to place a soft kiss on his cheek, her only response was "Goodnight James," before the door was shut firmly in his face.

CHAPTER TWELVE

Meghan awoke with a start, what on earth was that noise? It took her a few moments to realise that it was music that she could hear, coming from somewhere inside her cottage. Curiosity piqued, Meghan threw off her sheet and swung her legs off of the bed, padding out to the sitting area, coming to a dead stop in the doorway.

"What on Earth?!" She gaped at the sight that greeted her. James, looking good enough to eat, squatted in the corner of the room, un-tangling a string of fairy lights. The jeans he wore clung to his thighs, stretching across his manhood and leaving nothing to the imagination, Meghan was at a loss for words, unable to tear her eyes away from him. God, how she wanted him, her traitorous breasts already peaked, nipples pushing through her thin nightshirt, heat pooling in her core. James turned slowly, noticing how Meghan licked her lips hungrily and grinned.

"Morning sunshine, I thought I would get these lights up for you, make it a little more magical in here," he walked past her into the small kitchenette, dropping a kiss on her mouth as he went past. Wait, what on Earth was going on here? This was so obviously *not* the James from yesterday.

"How are you feeling this morning? Coffee?" He held the coffee pot up as he asked, Meghan numbly nodding her head in agreement, confused into silence over his odd behaviour. "Come on, sit down." James pulled a chair out at the table for Meghan. "I wasn't sure what you would feel like eating for breakfast today, so I just made you some scrambled eggs, pancakes, oven-cooked bacon, baked beans, hash browns and toast," he brandished a plate in front of her face. "Start eat-ing, I'm just going to pop next door and get my medical bag so that I can double-check your vitals and make sure you aren't suffering any more ill effects of your adventure last night," he smiled down at her, the twinkle in his eyes assuring her that he was indeed joking. Meghan looked at her plate and picked up a slide of toast to nibble, not realising how hungry she actually was until she started eating, embarrassed to realise when James returned with his medical bag that she had absent-mindedly finished everything on her plate. "Good, you finished." James seemed pleased as he cleared her plate and set up his instruments.

"So, has anything changed from last night, or will I still live?" Meghan asked through a yawn as James finished checking her over.

"You will live, happily," he replied dryly, "come on, back to bed with you," he led her back through to her bedroom, ushering her into bed before covering her with a sheet. "You are still slightly dehydrated Meg, a side effect of the heat stroke, but otherwise perfectly fine. I want you to stay in bed for a couple of days, I'll let everyone know so that you aren't bothered by a string of visitors. You aren't to leave the cottage, Meg, doctor's orders. If you need anything, I will be in the sitting area." Meghan closed her eyes against the headache she had forming behind them, barely having time to register what James had just said before sleep claimed her. When she finally awoke again, it was to find a glass of iced cold water next to her bed, along with two ibuprofen and a note from James, letting her know that his mother was sitting with her for a spell while he and his dad went to tend to a neighbour who had injured himself felling trees, but that he should be back in time for dinner, should she start to miss him. Despite her throbbing head, Meghan smiled to herself. *If* she started to miss him, honestly! She already *did* miss him. Maybe she was wrong to turn him down? Not wanting to think about her feelings, or James, especially not James, she took the ibuprofen and went back to sleep.

The next time she opened her eyes the room was dark, and she was starving. Climbing from the bed she tiptoed across the cool tiled floor through the sitting room into the kitchenette, opening the fridge to peer inside.

"If you are hungry, there is roast lamb warming in the oven along with some roast vegetables, courtesy of mum." James's soft voice spoke from the darkness, scaring Meghan half to death. She spun around, hand over her heart, gasping. "Sorry, I didn't mean to scare you," he eased his frame into the kitchenette, pulling her into his strong arms, cheering on the inside when she didn't resist him. "How are you feeling?"

"The ibuprofen helped, thank you." She breathed deeply, savouring the scent that was so uniquely him, the smell of sandalwood and antiseptic, committing it to her memory, knowing that she would remember it for years to come. "The lamb sounds delicious, are you planning on joining me?" She moved away from James's embrace, busying herself with pulling out plates and cutlery for the small table. With a slow sexy smile at Meghan, James assured her he would. After they had finished their meal, James gathered up all the pots and pans and took them back up to the main house, returning to find Meghan already sound asleep.

"Goodnight Meg," he bent to brush a kiss across her lips, struck with the feeling that he liked taking care of her, he liked this domesticity with her. He whistled as he walked back up to the house, he needed to talk to his dad about something important.

The following day started out in much the same way, although Meghan was feeling far less tired, and a lot more irritated with James's constant attention, a fact he found highly amusing.

"I don't know why you are so happy today," Meghan grumbled, glowering at him from her perch on the sofa. She was well and truly sick of being confined to this cottage, as pretty as it was. James refused to let her go wandering off, saying that she needed to rest after her adventure, but Meghan was starting to suspect that he had an ulterior motive. Every time she suggested they join his family for a meal or a visit, he had a reason as to why they couldn't possibly. He was starting to drive her mad and she wished she could have a few moments alone, even if she was secretly thrilled with all of the attention that he was lavishing on her.

"Really Meg, have you forgotten what day it is?" James moved her feet off the sofa and sat, pulling them onto his lap and starting to rub them.

"Saturday?" Meghan guessed, trying hard to focus on anything except the way James's hands were caressing her feet and calves.

"Meg," James was incredulous, he couldn't believe Meghan had forgotten. "Matt and Xavier arrive sometime later today, or maybe early tomorrow, it really depends on when they leave Alice Springs".

"Well then," Meghan cooed, a saccharine-sweet smile on her face, "don't you think you should go and get things ready for them?"

"Actually, it is already done. While you were busy sleeping the morning away," he teased, "we aired out and set up their cottages. They will be staying in the two cottages that are closest to the house."

"What? I thought that they would be staying in your cottage with you?" Meghan teased, enjoying James's look of horror.

"Good heavens no! The three of us shared a place together while we were at university, that was enough, believe me." James shuddered at the memory. "Anyway, I fully intend to spend every night with you, and they would only cramp my style." Meghan laughed out loud at this declaration, a giddy laugh that captivated James. "This is nice Meg, being with you, hearing you laugh." James took her hands in his. "Meg, will you spend the night with me? After we spend the day with my family, will you come back to my cottage with me, will you let me spend the evening with you?"

Listening to him, Meghan knew that she wouldn't refuse him, she wanted this, no matter what the next few months held, she wanted this. "Yes James, I will spend every evening we have left with you."

The rest of the day passed in a happy blur with Meghan spending most of it tucked up in bed while James pottered around the cottage, bringing her food and fluffing her pillows. In the early afternoon, there was a commotion of car doors shutting and scores of voices all clamouring to be heard over each other, Matthew and Xavier had arrived, and were welcomed as if they were returning from war. It was obvious that James's family considered them to be an extension of him, another brother, son and uncle to fawn and fuss over. Once they were settled into their accommodation, James's mother sent Xavier and Matthew down to Meghan's cottage with a note for James, telling him to stop hogging Meghan, and that they were both expected to be at the house no later than four o'clock. Matthew and Xavier happily teased James over this bit of information, which he took in his stride, knowing it was good-natured and done from a place of familiarity and love. Having heard the story of Meghan's bush adventure, as the family seemed determined to call it, Meghan was happy to assure them both that she was feeling fine now and ushered all three of them out of her cottage, telling Matthew and Xavier not to worry about bringing James back, that she would meet them all at the house at four o'clock, promising not to get lost, a statement that brought laughter from all three of them.

At exactly four o'clock, Meghan rounded the corner from the cottages to the house and was greeted by a cacophony of shouts and a rush of small bodies as James's nieces and nephews all scrambled to wrap tiny arms around her waist. Tears sprung unbidden to her eyes, she hadn't realised just how much she had missed James's family, even though she had only known them for such a short time, she had come to treasure them all. Meghan dropped to her knees and flung her arms wide, falling to the grass in a flurry of giggles and excited squawks. An animated Samuel, Gabby, Micah and Ella were busying telling her every little thing that had happened in the house during the past two days; Annie and Ella were demonstrating their cartwheels; Charley, Hunter and Piper, budding doctors, wanted to know if Meghan's head was better or if they needed to get her a bandage; Jerry, Emma and Georgina were trying to drag the family dogs over to join the excited group; and sweet Joe had brought Meghan a gift, a lizard in a jar. Meghan laughed at the craziness of it all, oh how she would miss this happy noise, this sense of belonging. Meghan was spared from having to hurt Joe's feelings by

James, who thankfully intercepted the lizard, declaring it a beauty, before extending his hand to help Meghan up off the ground.

Meghan wasn't sure who was more surprised, James or her, when she reached up and kissed him, before heading into the house with the kids following along behind.

"So, something has very obviously happened between the two of you," Matthew started, "is there anything you want to share with us?" Matthew, Xavier and James had been placed on barbecue duty, James suspected that it was a careful ploy on his mother's part to get the three of them out of her kitchen so that she could have some time alone with Meghan and his sisters, goodness knows what they were up to, he could hear bursts of laughter drifting through the kitchen window as they gossiped away, making whatever plots and plans it was that women made the night before an anniversary dinner. James turned the steaks over while he thought about Matthew's question. He knew he could trust the two of them to keep his secret, that was never in question, he trusted them with his life, literally. That wasn't the reason he hesitated, stalling for as long as he could. No, he wanted to keep his precious secret to himself for a purely selfish reason, he wasn't ready for it to become public knowledge just yet.

James turned to look at Xavier and Matthew. "What, a guy can't have his secrets?"

"No!" They answered in unison.

"Fine." James laughingly surrendered, crossing to sit in the wicker chair next to his friends, taking a swig of his homemade lemonade while he gathered his thoughts, checking to ensure no one else would overhear what he was about to say before he continued. "We had a fight, of epic proportions. I accused her of preferring to be alone as it was easier, she accused me of hiding from relationships," he coughed uneasily, "she, ah, was right, actually." His friends remained unusually quiet, and James was faced with an uncomfortable thought. "You knew?! You knew and you didn't say anything?"

Xavier shifted uneasily. "That's not entirely true," he started, "I told you that you should ask Meghan out," he finished helpfully. James knew his anger at his friends was misplaced, they had tried on numerous occasions to get him out and meet people, but each time he had brushed them off, preferring his own company, until now.

"I acted like a jerk, to be honest, I thought she might never speak to me again."

"So," Matthew probed, "what happened? If that kiss is anything to go by, you two are obviously very much back on speaking terms." James took a steadying breath and told his friends the entire story, leaving nothing out, safe in the conviction that his confession would not be mocked or judged, just listened to.

"Have you told Meghan yet, how you feel?" Xavier asked softly, slightly in awe of his friend. Who would ever have thought that James would act in such a manner, so unlike his usual measured and considered persona? He was impressed, for once James had gone after exactly what it was that he had wanted.

"No," James admitted. "I want to do it after mum and dad's anniversary lunch." At Matthew's and Xavier's frowns, James hastened to explain. "I want her to have a nice break here, and if she says no, neither of us will enjoy it." There, he had told them. He was worried about Meghan's reaction when he told her how he felt, and he was worried about his own reaction, to her answer. He knew he wouldn't be very pleasant to be around if Meghan turned him down, again.

The barbecue had been a lovely way to spend the evening, Meghan decided as she lay in bed later, the warmth of the night washing over her. Together with James's mother and sisters, they had finalised most of the plans for the anniversary lunch the day after tomorrow, which Meghan had thought quietly to herself seemed a bit more like a military operation than a celebration. She smiled at the thought of just how busy they would all be tomorrow, a happy busy. Meghan could hardly believe that it was already the third week of the month, that the month was nearly over for another year. A thought, unbidden, danced around the edges of Meghan's mind, refusing to come into focus. She had a feeling that there was something that she was supposed to do, but for the life of her, she couldn't remember what it was. *Well*, she reasoned with herself, *it obviously isn't that important, or she would be able to remember it.*

Meghan rose slowly as a wave of nausea washed over her. She felt awful, disorientated and shaky, unable to recall the last time that she was actually sick outside of her migraines, and hoped that no one else was feeling unwell today, not when there was so much to be done. She managed to make it through to the kitchenette where, hands shaking, she prepared herself a strong cup of tea, sitting down and sipping it slowly, which is where James found her when he stopped by on his way up to the house.

"Meg, are you okay? You look..." he searched for the right word, "pale." Meghan tried a smile that came out as a grimace, opened her mouth to speak, changed her mind and clamped her hand over her mouth, sprinting for the bathroom, she was going to be sick. Once she was finished, Meghan scrubbed her teeth and washed her face, opening the door to a concerned-looking James.

"I feel better now," she smiled wanly, "honestly, please don't worry. I probably should not have had a third helping of the chocolate mousse, it is a huge weakness of mine," she confessed guiltily. "I'm going to have a shower and then come up to the house," she stroked his cheek before resting her head against his chest as his arms encased her.

"I'll wait for you." She knew he would.

Meghan could not remember enjoying making breakfast this much in a long time, having pitched in to help make stacks of pancakes. Her emerald green summer dress was currently decorated with a liberal splattering of flour, ginger, and edible glitter, her hands damp with melted butter. She used her forearm to brush her hair off of her forehead, jumping as an arm snaked around her waist, James's head coming to rest on her shoulder. "Mmm, you smell...Edible," he teased her softly, enjoying watching her face flush under his gaze. "Meg," he whispered, lips pressed to her ear, his breath fanning her face. "Come...With me," her eyes widening at his double entendre, his hand moved slightly to brush against the side of her breast, "I want to show you something." Meghan glanced around the large kitchen, everyone busily involved with their own tasks, not paying the slightest bit of attention to her and James. Nodding her head in agreement she placed the rolling pin she had been using on the bench, reaching for the tap. "Oh no," her hand was caught by James who entwined it with his own. "I want you just the way you are, perfect."

He led her through the fenced yard and past the barn, following a path that was all too familiar to him, bringing her to a stop beside an apple tree in a secluded area next to the creek.

"Oh James," Meghan gasped delightedly at the sight that greeted her, a chequered picnic blanket spread out, holding an array of scatter pillows, a picnic breakfast set up for the two of them. "It is gorgeous!"

"Meg," James slid his free arm around her waist, drawing her to him. "I fully intend to kiss you now," he warned, eyes darkening, lowering his head slowly to give her the chance to stop him if she chose to. Not that she could have, her legs felt as stable as jelly, her heart racing, pulse quickening.

"James," her voice thick with longing, "I fully intend to let you." His mouth crashed down against hers, needing no more encouragement, his senses delighting in tasting her, his every thought drowning in her. His hand slipped down over her backside, sliding back up under her dress to cup her soft cheek, feeling her bare skin on his hand, groaning in delight as he kneaded her flesh, pressing her tight against his arousal, needing to feel her against him, wanting her closer, surrounding him.

With a great amount of difficulty, he broke the kiss, smoothing Meghan's dress back down and grinning at her sheepishly, answering the question in her eyes. "I wasn't exactly planning on a full-blown seduction Meg, only a nice picnic," he shrugged, "I didn't bring any precautions with me," he apologised.

"Never apologise for protecting me, James." Meghan kissed him thoroughly, hoping to tell him without words just how much she appreciated his thoughtfulness, his protection of her, just how much she ached for his touch. "Well then, I shall just have to look forward to tonight," she smiled delightedly, turning her attention to the picnic set out for the two of them. They breakfasted on ham and cheese croissants and fresh fruit salad, washed down with a thermos of the most delicious homemade iced tea that Meghan had ever tasted. James thought that their dessert had been the best part, having smuggled out two of his mother's elaborately decorated cupcakes, enjoying watching Meghan's delight as she bit into the chocolate peppermint devil's food cake. Yes, he decided as he watched her lick a stray crumb off her top lip with the tip of her tongue, definitely worth his mother's wrath.

James walked Meghan back to the house slowly, relishing in just being with her, surprising her when he made to come inside with her.

"What," she teased lightly, "no more guy stuff to do?"

"Just wait," he steered her through the kitchen into the dining room, where his entire family were waiting, the large dining room table littered with boxes of photographs, scissors of varying styles, and pots of glue at each place setting. "Surprise! Every year for their anniversary my parents arrange a family project, we all pitch in and make something, and then it goes into the house to be used and admired." Whatever James might have expected Meghan's reaction to be, it was not this.

"That is so romantic!" Utter delight danced across her face, eyes glittering, she threw her arms around his neck with a force so strong he nearly toppled over, staggering them backwards to keep his balance. "Thank you for letting me share this with you."

James explained that previous years had seen them plant a rose garden; brick in a barbecue pit; and build the dining room table and chairs. His parents had never purchased gifts for each other, preferring to make something meaningful. This year, his parents had decided that they wanted a photo gallery, not content to merely display them, framed, on the shelf anymore. One of the rooms in the main house had been stripped bare, and they were intending that the entire wall surface be covered in photographs. Everyone was to choose the ones they loved best, decorate them or embellish them as they saw fit, and then add them to the pile to be attached to the wall later that afternoon. Meghan thought it sounded like a wonderful way to celebrate an anniversary. They spent the most enjoyable afternoon, surrounded by his family, each decorating their own pile of photographs, Meghan enjoyed seeing some of James's early days.

There were snips of photographs and blobs of dried glue from one end of the table to the other, and enough assorted craft supplies to stock the world's best craft shop, twice over. The result of their labours was an interesting and varied bunch of photographs, with some photographs, like James's choices, dripping in so much glitter and sparkle dust that the sides had already started to curl up,

and others, like a few of the children's chosen photographs, so bereft of any decorations or alterations that Meghan knew they would find glitter all over themselves instead. Meghan's was different again; she had forgone the glitter glue in preference for cutting shapes out of her favourite photographs, outlining the edges and drawing doddle hearts and kisses on the photographs with paint pens. She added her name to the bottom of the photograph, at Zonja's request, and leant back, smiling at her work. Zonja thought it would be a nice idea to show everyone the completed room tomorrow at her anniversary lunch, and Meghan had thought it a lovely idea. Once all of the photographs were complete and boxed up on the bench to await their installation, the adults hurried to tidy the dining room and shoo hyped-up children through the chore of scrubbing their hands free of glitter and glue, ushering them outside to run off their excess energy before they would be called into lunch.

The afternoon passed in a blur of work, everyone helping attach the photographs to the walls. The work would have been a lot quicker if people didn't keep stopping to laugh and point out a funny alteration made. An anniversary eve dinner, as Meghan found out, was just as important in the Cristo household as the actual anniversary dinner. As the tangerine sun spread its final rays across the barren landscape, excitement filled the main house as bodies big and small moved in all directions, adding last-minute touches to the already heavily laden dining table, straightening ties and organising the younger members through showers and into their outfits already laid out on their beds. Meghan slipped back to her cottage to shower and change, donning an outfit that she had brought just for the occasion, a knee-length open back halter top sea-green soft organza dress, that floated and swirled as she walked. Meghan had seen it in a local Alice Springs dress shop and had fallen in love with it. She paired it with a pair of emerald-green rhinestone ballet flats that sparkled in the light, a touch of her nude lip gloss, and a spritz of her favourite perfume. When James arrived at her door to escort her back up to the main house for dinner, he was momentarily speechless, a slow heat unfurling inside of him, spreading slowly throughout his loins as he openly assessed her, his gaze lazily stretching down the length of her body before journeying back up again. Heaven help him, he had no idea how he would make it through dinner intact when she looked that good, that delectable.

If James appeared flustered throughout dinner no one commented on it. Seated next to Meghan, her delicate hand having slipped down beneath the table, coming to rest on his upper thigh, creeping slowly upwards to unexpectedly cup his manhood through his linen pants and squeezing gently, causing him to drop his fork with a thunderous crash onto his plate, earning a few concerned frowns. As Meghan's hand continued to tease him, massaging him with her deft fingers, he gritted his teeth and tried to concentrate on what it was that he was eating. When he dropped his fork for the third time, Meghan, innocence personified, looked at him with concern etched across her face, cupping his face gently, asking him "Honey, are you okay? You seem distracted." Leaning across to place a kiss on his cheek, she spoke low into his ear, "I forgot to tell you, I am completely naked under this dress," enjoying seeing his face drain of colour as he struggled to swallow. She patted his cheek and returned back to enjoying her dinner, how she was able to hold up a fluid conversation with anyone James wasn't sure, he was barely able to swallow and if he had been asked later, he would not have been able to name a single thing that he had eaten, such was his distraction.

James couldn't move. Watching Meghan swirl across the room and disappear into the kitchen, her dress moving against her thighs as she walked, had put him in a very awkward position. Knowing that the only thing between him and her soft flesh was a scrap of flimsy fabric didn't help matters any, and so he sat there, at the dining table, discussing the possibility of genetically altering a crop of pineapples to create a new species, one without any outer thorns, having instead, smooth skin similar to a banana. He knew that he must appear stark raving mad to his family, having never been *this* interested in his brother in laws line of work before, and not fully understanding what it even was that Daniel even actually did, apart from knowing that it was something science related. He shifted uncomfortably, feigning interest, asking Daniel to elaborate, not needing to pretend that he had no idea what Daniel was actually talking about, ignoring the bemused expressions that Xavier and Matthew were viewing him with from across the table.

"So, dinner was...interesting." Matthew placed a lot of emphasis on the last word. It was only through sheer willpower that James had made it through dinner and the lingering dessert, all but sprinting from the house once his issue had flagged, the cooling night air a blessed relief on the heat of his skin. He was slumped in a wicker chair flanked by Matthew and Xavier, trying not to think about Meghan, waiting for her to finish saying her goodbyes so that he could take her back to his cottage and show her exactly how that had felt. Yes, he grinned to him-self, his revenge would be so sweet.

"I am not sure I have ever seen you *that* awkward around a girl since our first week at university." Xavier ribbed, thoroughly enjoying James's discomfort.

"It must have been the dress Meghan was wearing," Matthew sup-plied faux innocently.

"Oh, and here was I thinking it was her talent for eating one-hand-ed," Xavier deadpanned, before both he and Matthew dissolved into peals of laughter.

"Shut up!" James glared at his friend, horrified at the thought that they knew what he had been going through.

"Ah, here she is," Xavier gestured towards Meghan, stepping out of the doorway, framed in a pool of light. "Have a nice evening you two, we'll see you in the morning." Meghan suppressed a smile, certain that they knew, if James's fluster was anything to go on. They strolled slow-ly back to the cottage, surprising Meghan, she had throught that James would be frantic to get her inside and out of this dress. James opened the door to his cottage, sweeping Meghan into his arms and lifting her across the threshold, spinning her around with a giddy excitement be-fore depositing her in the sitting room. He advanced on her with hood-ed eyes, slowly discarding his jacket, removing his tie, and releasing the buttons on his shirt, never breaking eye contact. Her tongue darted out to slide across her bottom lip, eyes darkening with lust, breasts heaving with her ragged breath. He released his fly, his linen pants falling to the ground, his erection clearly visible through the satin of the boxer shorts he wore.

One more step, Meghan thought to herself, her body already quiv-ering in anticipation. Just one more step and he would be able to touch her. Smiling, James advanced slowly in a wide arc, walking around Meghan, coming to stop directly in front of her. Without preamble he crushed her lithe body to his, capturing her bottom lip between his teeth, biting down gently before sucking, his hand gripping the fabric of her dress over her buttocks, balling it up in his hand, pushing it out of the way, laughing in delight at the discovery of her being panty less. "You little minx! You have no idea just how hard dinner was for me." He slid his hand between her buttocks at the apex of her thighs, dragging it back slowly, feeling her dripping wetness, how wet she already was for him, her core pulsing with desire. Leaving his hand there, cupping her sex, he trailed his mouth down to her breast, latching onto it through the fabric of her dress, suckling until her nipple puckered beneath his mouth, rolling the hardened nib around his mouth, flicking it with his tongue, nipping at it with his teeth as Meghan arched her back and thrashed below him, whimpering his name in desperation.

Breaking away from her with a ragged breath, he pulled her dress up and over her head in a single fluid motion, tossing it aside, his boxer shorts joining it moments later, his erection jutting out proudly for all to see. James gathered her into his arms and carried her through to the bedroom, depositing her on a bed surrounded by trailing ivy leaves, the sight of her splayed out as if in some secret garden almost his undoing. He ripped open a condom and sheathed himself before joining her on the bed, scooping her legs up over his shoulders, he plunged into her without preamble, sinking down into her deepness. Meghan gasped as James stabbed into her, his length always surprised her, her body stretching to accommodate him. There was a feral need between them tonight, a hunger that couldn't be sated, as she clung to him, her fingers gripping against his broad shoulders, his generous length growing even longer still as he stabbed into her shaking core again and again. Their release, when it came, was explosive, rolling spasms that anchored him inside her, their mutual shouts of triumph filling the air around them.

He hated to leave her, enjoyed the feeling of her warmth wrapped around him, the way they fit so perfectly together. She feathered touches up and down his strong arms and across his back, smattering kisses across his chest, loving the way he felt inside her, the way that he was already hard again. Lifting one of her legs up to grip the bed, Meghan gave a push, rolling them both over. With James still nestled deep inside of her, Meghan guided his hand up to her sensitive nub, giggling delightedly as he began to swirl and roll it between his thumb and forefinger, pulling it lightly, then pinching it with a sharp twist, shooting spasms of pleasure to her very core. Splaying her legs even wider and arching her back, Meghan reached behind her to hold onto James's calves, giving him an uninterrupted view of her straddling him to the hilt, his sensitive balls flanking her molten core. James knew that no matter how long he lived, he would never see anything hotter than what he was seeing right now. He raised his knees and moved into a sitting position, his mouth plundering Meghan's, his free hand twisting and pinching her nipple in time with the ministrations to her sensitive nub.

Meghan moaned into James's mouth, her entire body was tingling with delight, humming with a need only he could satisfy. She knew they were close, she wanted to see his face, to see what she could do to him. Breaking away from the kiss she pushed him firmly back down against the bed, sighing contentedly when his hand continued to torment her breast, delighting in the sensations he elicited from her peaked nipples. Smiling lazily, she leant down to touch his balls, a gasp escaping her lips as James bucked involuntarily beneath her, plunging even deeper into her. His hands released her, moving to grip her hips, tethering her to him, keeping his erection firmly positioned in her aching centre. Meghan moved her hips in small circles, rolling his balls in her hot hands, her nub rubbing against James's pelvic bone, fissions of heat coiling up her body. James bucked and ground into her from below, Meghan lifting her hips and meeting them thrust for thrust. When he was almost there, Meghan released his balls, and looking James straight in the eye, slipped her hand in between their bodies and gave her nub a hard tweak, shooting spasms of pleasure to her very core, sending them both over the edge with such force Meghan was sure her heart had stopped beating. Hours later, both completely spent, James held her as she slept, curled into his side, completely naked, body entwined with his.

It was a surreal feeling, Meghan decided, to wake up in James's arms.

"Good morning," she kissed him, feeling him stir beneath her. "Really?" she asked, secretly delighted with his response.

"I am insatiable for you," he answered simply, drawing her closer and deepening their kiss, relishing in spending the next hour showing her, again, just how insatiable for her he really was. Satisfied that he had proven his point, James relaxed against the bedhead, watching as Meghan strode around picking up her clothes, putting them on haphazardly, unconcerned with her appearance, certain that no one would be around to see her walk back to her own cottage. Meghan hurried through her shower, the last thing she wanted was for the rest of the family to be waiting any longer than they had to for them to arrive, besides, she was starving and keen to get into breakfast. Opening her door to James, Meghan was greeted by a low whistle of appreciation.

"Gorgeous," he eyed her longingly. "There is just one thing missing," he stated, presenting her with a small velvet box tied with a red bow.

"James!" Meghan gasped in surprise, as she accepted it with shaky hands, fumbling as she opened it to reveal the moonstone necklace nestled on a bed of deep blue satin.

"It is gorgeous!" James pulled Meghan into his arms, turning her around to face the mirror next to the front door, taking the necklace from her hands, fastening it around her neck, the moonstone pendant nestling into the hollow in her throat.

"When I this necklace Meg, I knew I wanted you to have it," he swallowed the lump in his throat. "I knew I wanted to be the one to give it to you Meg." Turning in his arms, Meghan rested her head against his chest, listening to the sound of his heart beating, the steady cadence of the thud, thud, thud. "Meg," he lifted her chin with his finger, looking deep into her eyes. "I love you. I am *in* love with you." Breath catching in her throat, tears pooling in her eyes, Meghan opened her mouth to reply, stopped by the sudden opening of the front door as a gaggle of James's nieces and nephews streamed in.

It had been an insufferably long morning for James. Surrounded by chattering kids, he and Meghan had been unable to finish their conversation, her eyes assuring him that it was okay, that she would come to him later, but he had been on edge all day. Even a hearty breakfast of his favourite items didn't soothe him. Meghan, sensing his unease, hadn't left his side all morning and was presently curled up next to him, her head resting on his shoulder, as they watched the chaos of his parents unwrapping their anniversary gifts unfold. James's mother had been giddy with excitement when, having commented on Meghan's necklace, she learnt that it had been a gift from James himself. James had been surprised when Meghan had moved from his side, to hand out variously shaped rectangular boxes to everyone, not just his parents. His curiosity piqued, he opened his box, floored to find a stunning black and white photo of him, Matthew and Xavier, concentration etched across their faces as they looked at a case file. He remembered this night, they had been researching a medical condition at the hospital library and lost track of the time, and Meghan had come to find them. The photo had managed to capture the three of them perfectly, and James was touched by her gift.

Matthew and Xavier, along with his father and sisters had also received identical gifts, and the children, while receiving photo frames, had been given colourful, goofy photos of their uncle James, taken one evening by Meghan after a horrid day at work, claiming that she needed to blow off steam. The children all thought them especially funny, swapping them around so that everyone could have a look. It was James's mother that surprised everyone, bursting burst into tears when she opened her gift, the room falling silent as she tried to regain her composure, waving away everyone's concern, assuring them all that she loved her gift, that she was just being silly. She crossed the room and enveloped Meghan in a hug so fierce and long, that no one could tear their eyes away, James's dad eventually prying his wife away from Meghan with an awkward laugh. When asked, she refused to reveal her gift, instead leaving the room to place it somewhere safe, away from prying eyes, returning with a beaming smile that couldn't be dimmed.

Sitting down to their family anniversary lunch, James smiled at his family, laughing at the silly jokes and passing around platters laden down with food. His mother had insisted that Meghan be seated between her and Arabella, which put her directly across from James, he was aware of her every move, aware that every time he looked at her, she was smiling at him. James sensed that something had shifted between him and Meghan, he felt the well of possibility bubbling away inside of him and was keen to get her out of his parent's house and back to their earlier conversation, certain that she would tell him of her reciprocated feelings. Halfway through lunch, there was a loud knock on the front door, silencing conversation instantly, everyone glancing towards the hallway. Who on earth would be knocking on their door at this time of the day? They certainly were not expecting anyone. Dread filled James, the only reason someone would come knocking at lunchtime on a ranch would be if there had been an accident, their neighbouring properties around here all knowing that the Cristo property maintained a working runway capable of landing a Royal Flying Doctor Service aircraft. Xavier and Matthew rose in unison with James, all having had the same thoughts. Pulling open the front door, they were met, not with an anxious neighbour as they had thought, but with Jessinta, James's ex-girlfriend.

"Hello, James".

CHAPTER THIRTEEN

Face as dark and as grim as a thundercloud, James strode back into the dining room, followed by an anxious Matthew and Xavier, both gesturing wildly behind James's back. "We have a...Guest." James gritted his teeth as he said the last word, spitting it out with obvious effort, his family looking up in surprise that gave way to incredulity and finally ended with dislike and, in his parent's case, hatred. Sitting back down, James drained his wine glass in a single mouthful, ignoring the way his family all shot worried glances at each other, and between Meghan and James. Damn! Meghan didn't even know who this was yet, was blissfully unaware that her so far perfectly happy day was about to be ruined in spectacular fashion.

"Oh James," Jessinta trilled, "I am hardly a guest"

"Jessinta," James ground out, ignoring Meghan's shocked gasp as she recognised the name, "for once, I am in complete agreeance with you." It was, James thought, the most uncomfortable meal of his life. Jessinta, having helped herself to a kitchen chair and placing it ridiculously close to James's at the dining table. If looks could kill, Jessinta would have been cremated under his mother's gaze. The rest of the meal passed in absolute silence, even the usually boisterous children were mute little statues. The silence would have been deafening if it hadn't been for the scraping of cutlery against the china plates, and the incessant rattling on by Jessinta, who seemed oblivious to the tension she had caused in the room.

James clenched and unclenched his jaw, the muscle there working overtime. Meghan after learning of Jessinta's name, had not taken her eyes off her dinner plate, apparently fascinated with her meal of roast beef, a stunned look on her face. James couldn't quite look Meghan in the eye, and everyone else was watching Jessinta with varying degrees of annoyance and downright hatred. Jessinta, making no attempt at all to hide her brazen actions, moved her hand to rest against James's upper thigh, dangerously close to his crotch, squeezing gently, the way a lover would. As James's cutlery crashed down to his plate, dropped in shock, Meghan jumped, looking across at him and Jessinta, eyes widening at the scene in front of her, her face growing pale as she drew the same conclusion as everyone else sitting at the table. Standing up so fast that her chair overbalanced and crashed to the floor with a deafening thud, Meghan stood, rooted to the spot, Arabella coming to her rescue by exclaiming that she was sure that Meghan had not left the oven on, but that they should go and check, just in case.

Linking arms with Meghan, Arabella guided her through to the bedroom that she was using at the back of the house, well away from prying eyes and big ears, carefully closing the door firmly behind them. Meghan sat on the edge of Arabella's bed and looked up at her, anguish in her eyes. "Did you see that?" her voice barely a whisper. "Her hands were all over him." A single tear slid slowly down her cheek.

"He loves you, Meghan, I am sure of it." Arabella *had* been sure of it until Jessinta walked back through the door. She knew that her brother had unfinished business with that woman, knew that she wasn't the only one worried about her influence over James, remembering all too well just what had happened the last time they had parted, how her parents were not sure James would ever get over her, ever be willing to take another chance at settling down, at happiness. Then he had brought Meghan home for their anniversary, and they had all known, this woman, she was the one, she was his ever after, even if it appeared that neither James nor Meghan knew it themselves.

Adamant that she was not going to hide away and feel sorry for herself, Meghan crossed to the bathroom and washed her face, running into eight-year-old Emma, who begged to be able to do a makeover on her, having been given a play makeup set for her recent birthday from her doting Grandma, and desperate to use it today. Shrugging, Meghan agreed, that it would be nice to just sit and close her eyes for a few moments. Once Emma was done, Meghan glanced in the mirror and smiled. One thing was obvious, Emma certainly loved colour! Meghan offered to do Emma's face in return, and the two of them walked back into the dining room flaunting their new looks.

"Oh, good grief, what happened to your face?" Jesinta burst into laughter, grasping James's bicep for support, at the sight of Meghan and Emma.

Eyes narrowing at Jessinta's familiarity with James, Meghan draped an arm around Emma's shoulders, pulling her closer to her side. "It's called a makeover, Jessinta." Then, placing an index finger on her chin as if she was thinking, added thoughtfully, "If only they had those for personalities." The insult was sadly lost on Jessinta, not so on anyone else, his father particularly amused, nearly choking on his drink, Matthew jumping up and slapping him on the back until he calmed back down, tears coursing down his weathered cheeks.

James somehow made it through the rest of the meal, and then dessert, all the while on edge, unable to relax, even for a minute, his mind going through the various reasons that he could think of for why Jessinta would be here. As the last of the dishes were cleared from the table, and knowing that he had no choice, that he couldn't very well make her sleep in her car, and that everywhere else in the nearest town would be booked solid, he begrudgingly invited Jessinta to stay, not missing the hurt look on Meghan's face, or the way her entire body was stiff with the stress of the day. Sighing, James stood, slipping a key from the hook on the wall and walking out the front door, past Jessinta's suitcase. Let her carry her own damn bag. He marched across to the nearest cottage, unlocking the door and handing the key to Jessinta, turning to leave, not caring if it was made up or not.

"James, wait," there was an uncertainty to Jessinta's voice and James found himself stopping and looking back.

"What?" he snapped, crossing his arms over his chest in a defensive move.

"We need to talk James. Please," she placed her hand on his forearm. "That's what I came here for, please just hear me out and I will leave first thing in the morning."

James really did not want to hear whatever it was that Jessinta had come to say. How dare she show up unannounced, how dare she show up at all, and on his parent's anniversary! James shook his head in disbelief at her, wondering if he had ever actually known her at all. Whether she knew it or not, Jessinta had ruined the plans that James had had for the rest of the day, the plans he had made for Meghan, and he knew, as much as it ached him to have to admit it, he knew that Meghan would now not be willing to finish their earlier conversation. James thought he would be lucky if she ever spoke to him again. He gave Jessinta a long hard look, noticing how she had changed, she seemed calmer somehow. "Jessinta, you are stuck here until tomorrow. If you feel the need to talk things over, feel free, but do not, for one second, expect me to change my plans in any way to accommodate you. It is my parent's anniversary, and in case you haven't noticed, I am at home with my family. So, talk, talk until you are hoarse if it makes you feel better, but you will need to do it around our festivities."

Expecting her to remain in her cottage and sulk, James was stunned to see Jessinta walk back through the door, and actually join his family in the lounge room, where they were playing an especially competitive game of charades, his parents on opposing teams, the winning team responsible for serving tonight's dinner, and the clean up afterwards. It was a family tradition that had carried over from James's childhood, only now his parents divided up the remaining guests to bolster the teams, making the job a lot easier than it was when it was just the kids to help. When James had first come back from escorting Jessinta to her cottage, the teams had already been decided, and as much as he had chafed to sit next to Meghan, she had circumvented his plans by seating herself between his mother and Arabella, hands clenched in her lap. Which was how he found himself sitting next to Jessinta, on his father's team, watching Meghan from afar. She might have only been across the room, but as far as James was concerned, she may well have been on the other side of the world.

Meghan smiled until she felt that her face would break, determined to pretend, as well as she could, that everything was okay. She still could not comprehend what had happened, Jessinta was here, Jessinta, James's ex-girlfriend, was actually here, in his parent's house. She was pretty, beautiful actually, Meghan conceded, and, as she discovered during a round of charades, she was a Royal Flying Doctor Service flight nurse. That was how she had met James, they had worked together for years. As Meghan watched James, she wondered if he knew how he looked with Jessinta, if he knew how perfect they looked together. Meghan wondered what James was thinking when he lent into Jessinta, head bowed to hear what she was saying, staring into her face before nodding once, and excusing himself from the game, following Jessinta from the room.

The game had all but stalled once James and Jessinta left the house, Zonja bursting into tears and going off to her room to lie down, not able to comprehend her only son's behaviour. Gerhardus followed his wife, shaking his head sadly and muttering about throwing away a perfectly good thing. The rest of the adults broke up into smaller groups, scattering throughout the house, Meghan found herself listlessly sitting next to the pool, longing for the solitude of her own cottage, but too polite to feel comfortable leaving just yet. Gabby came to find her, snuggling up at her side, showing off her new picture book, which Meghan read to her, before allowing Gabby to lead her through to the kitchen, joining Arabella in organising some dinner for everyone, leftovers and dinner rolls, finger foods, buffet style. Although everyone, with the very noticeable exception of James and Jessinta, came to the dinner table when called, no one had any real enthusiasm for eating, and Meghan, unable to continue to pretend that she was okay, stood slowly, shoulders slumped, a sad smile gracing her face. "I'm sorry, I can't do this," she spoke softly, every word a goodbye, walking away from a family she had grown to love.

Locking her door for the first time since she arrived, not wanting to see James, yet also fearful that he might not bother stopping by, Meghan encased herself in the safety of her cottage. Alone, at last, Meghan finally allowed herself to feel, heart-wrenching sobs wracking her entire body, shaking every fibre of her being, unable to stand the weight of her sadness any longer, Meghan collapsed across her bed, curling into the smallest ball she could, holding herself lest she break apart from the pain. She awoke sometime in the night, throat raw from crying, muscles stiff from having slept in such an odd position. No longer crying, she now only felt a numbing hole, it was as if her heart had been ripped out, a gaping chasm remaining in its place. She undid her dress, removing it and throwing it into the corner, heading for the bathroom. Standing there, the steam from the hot water filling the room, Meghan caught sight of her reflection in the mirror, a ghostly shadow of herself. She looked ill, the necklace James gave her still nestled at the base of her neck, taunting her. She struggled with the clasp, eventually getting it off, padding back through to the bedroom to throw it into her suitcase. Opening the lid, something caught her eye that made Meghan's blood run cold.

Meghan paced her cottage for the rest of the night, unable to fall back to sleep, willing daylight to come, tormenting herself with imagined visions of what James and Jessinta were getting up to. She wondered if he had stayed the night in her cottage, or whether he had taken her back to his cottage. Did he go back to the house? Was he surprised to find that Meghan wasn't waiting for him to return? Had he even remembered that Meghan was here? Had he told Jessinta that he loved her? It was this thought that was Meghan's undoing, the tears flowing again until she thought she would surely die. Meghan sat, staring out of the window, waiting until she had spied the first signs that the sky was changing from an inky blackness to a more pastel blue hue, before she moved, slipping on her shoes and heading out across the lawn, hoping that no one was up early enough to see her. She knocked on the door of Matthew's cottage softly, then louder, more insistent, until the door was opened, Matthew staring down at her through sleep-filled eyes. "Matthew, can I come in please," desperation tinged Meghan's question. "I need your help."

Sitting across from Matthew, a warm cup of tea in front of her, Meghan no longer felt very sure of herself. This was James's friend, his best friend. "I need some advice, but you can't tell James," at his conflicted look, she hurried to add, "medical advice. Please, Matthew, you have to promise me that you won't say anything to him, he can't know, he can't." Meghan knew she must look a mess, her eyes red and blotchy, voice hoarse from crying all night.

"If you are coming to me as a patient Meghan, whatever you say to me is in confidence, you have my word on that." Satisfied that Matthew was being honest with her, Meghan took a deep breath and dived right in.

"I think...I mean, I need to check...It's probably nothing," she couldn't stop the panic from creeping into her voice, Matthew looking at her with obvious worry etched across his face. "It is just that I, um," blushing furiously, Meghan stumbled forward. "It is just that I packed something that I thought I would have needed, in fact I *know* I should have needed it by now, but I haven't needed it, at all," she finished lamely, acutely embarrassed, never having been in this situation before.

"Meghan," realisation dawning on his face, "are you pregnant?"

Matthew waited while Meghan was in the bathroom, thoughts racing through his head. After Meghan had left last night, everyone else had slowly drifted off, only Xavier and Matthew had remained, waiting for James to return, unsure of just how their friend would be feeling. When midnight had come and gone and there was still no sign of James, Matthew and Xavier had agreed not to jump to any conclusions and had returned to their cottages, agreeing to speak with James first thing in the morning. But now, with Meghan's revelation, Matthew had to wonder just what the hell his friend was doing. Meghan reappeared and handed him a specimen jar, looking horribly nervous. Matthew wished there was something he could say to soothe her, but nothing came to mind. He ran the necessary test and set the timer on his phone, both of them sitting in silence until his phone beeped. Matthew looks at the test, reads the result, and then looks up at Meghan. "You're pregnant."

Meghan watches him studiously, the moment he looks up at her, she knows, she can see it in his face before he even opens his mouth to speak. Hearing him actually say it, actually confirm it in words though, is too much to bear and she succumbs to tears, shrugging off Matthew's attempts at sympathy, at calming her down, and returning instead to her own cottage.

She would ignore it, that's what she would do, Meghan decided, childishly placing both of her hands over her ears to block out the offending noise of voices talking outside of her cottage. Oh, how she would love to be able to go for a walk, to slip off somewhere quiet and sit, to think, but every time she went outside was just another chance to be tortured, humiliated, to see James with Jessinta. The voices didn't appear to be going anywhere and Meghan slipped closer to the window, ears straining. Gerhardus and Arabella, she realised, with a surge of disappointment erupting inside. How stupid could she be, Meghan thought bitterly. James hadn't come past to try and see her last night, nor at any time this morning, what the hell was wrong with her? Why was she still expecting him to? He had obviously made his choice, Meghan decided, a coldness spreading within her, he had chosen Jessinta, not Meghan. That's fine, she resolved to herself, just fine. At least now she knew the truth, that she had been a fill-in after all.

The last thing Meghan felt like doing was eating, convinced that she would not be able to swallow around the sawdust in her mouth, yet here she was, once again sitting at the dining room table in James's parent's house, staring down at a plate of food, her stomach churning at the thought. When Gerhardus and Arabella had asked her to join the family for breakfast, Meghan had not felt strong enough to argue and had accompanied them up to the house, not even bothering to stop and wash her face. The mood in the room was subdued, the table had been set up as it had been two nights ago, with the added chair for Jessinta, who had been placed at the head of the table, with Meghan's chair now back between James and Zonja. She had somehow managed to ignore the looks from everyone as she arrived and slipped into her chair, moving it as far away from James as possible without sitting in Zonja's lap, not even bothering to try and do it discreetly. Why should she? No, she wanted him to know, to see very clearly how much she did not want to be near him, the very thought making her skin crawl.

James could not take his eyes off her, he didn't care that he was openly staring, fixated, and obsessed. Every single thing about Meghan screamed at him, yelled that she was *not* happy, that she was furious with him. If her face was anything to go by, she had obviously been up all night, crying, the very thought twisted painfully inside, knotting his stomach. Had she waited for him? He had asked Xavier and Matthew the same thing when he had first seen them this morning, and they had looked at him with sad, disbelieving eyes, shaking their heads slowly. He had thought that by giving her some space last night, by not going to talk to her, that he would be giving her time to some time to calm down. Instead, she looked as if she may very well want to kill him. Unable to stand the scrutiny any longer, Meghan made to stand up, a wave of nausea washing over her. Calling out an apology, hand clamped over her mouth, Meghan made a run to the bathroom, only just making it. James looked at her plate, she hadn't eaten anything at all. James stood, intending to follow Meghan, but was stopped by Matthew, "I'll go."

"Meghan, can I get you anything?"

Meghan opened the bathroom door and smiled at Matthew, the smile not quite reaching her eyes. "No thank you," her tone was clipped, measured. "I'm fine, it was probably just something I ate."

"Meghan," Matthew's voice was soothing, a balm for her stretched nerves. "You need to tell him, James has a right to know, no matter what happened yesterday, you still need to tell him, before it is too late." James stopped dead in his tracks, about to step around the corner. Tell him what? Had something happened? Fear tugged at his heart, niggling away at him. Had something happened with Meghan and Matthew, had she seen him yesterday, turned to him for comfort?

"I know you are right," Meghan was saying now, "but I don't trust him. For all I know, he spent the night with her." James's heart constricted painfully at her bitter tone. She didn't trust him, Meghan actually thought that he had been with Jessinta all night. She thought he had been unfaithful to her, no wonder she looked so murderous. "I have to go and have a shower Matthew, I will tell James the next time I see him, okay?" James ducked out of the way, his mind reeling.

CHAPTER FOURTEEN

By the time Meghan had stood under the shower long enough for the hot water to start to run cold, she had started to feel slightly better. Not wanting to put it off any longer, she dressed in a plain navy-blue cotton shift dress and went to look for James, starting at his cottage next door. Finding that the front door was opened wide, Meghan walked in and stopped dead in her tracks, a strangled sob escaping her throat at the sight that greeted her. Jessinta had her arms wrapped tightly around James, her lips on his. Separated by the surprise interruption, two pairs of eyes looked up at Meghan, one set curious, the other horrified. Not wanting an explanation, not wanting to hear any lies from his mouth, with tears blinding her vision, Meghan turned on her heel and sprinted out of the door, back to her own cottage. Going straight through to her bedroom, Meghan opened her suitcase on her bed and started throwing her clothes inside. She would walk if she had to, but there was no way she was going to spend one more minute more than she had to in this place, near him. She had been such an idiot, to trust him, to fall in love with him, the thought shocking her. She loved him. She had fallen in love with him, despite her best efforts not to. Oh, dear heavens, what was she going to do now? How can she ever be strong enough to let him go?

"Meg, please, stop, let me explain." James touched her wrist, hoping to get her to stop her packing. Instead, she turned on him, a feral, furious glint in her eyes.

"Don't. You. Ever. Call. Me. That. Again," she hissed at him. "My name is Meghan."

"Nothing happened Meghan, please let me explain." James had never felt so out of his element before, so unsure of what to do or what to say. He knew that he owed her the truth, he also knew that this was it, whatever he said to her at this moment would most likely be the very last thing he ever said to her.

"Nothing happened?" Meghan sounded incredulous. "Do you honestly expect me to believe that? I saw you; you were kissing!"

"Meghan, ple-"

"Do you think I am stupid?" Meghan no longer cared about keeping her voice down, what difference did it make if everyone heard her or not. "So, was it everything you imagined it would be, James, make-up sex with your ex?"

"Meghan, don't," there was a warning in James's voice.

"Don't what? Talk about it? It's no secret that you spent last night with her James. Did you tell her about us?"

"Yes." James snapped. "Now, please, let me explain."

"That must have been some conversation, telling the love of your life about the fill-in that you enjoyed over the past couple of months."

"Fill in?!" James had had enough. "What about the speed at which you replaced me in your bed? Or does that not count?" James watched with a satisfied smile as her head shot up. Bingo, he *had* been right, and to think that he had actually imagined himself in love with this woman.

"What is that supposed to mean?" Meghan looked at him, her face pale, drained of all colour.

"Who are you to judge me, a bit hypocritical don't you think Meghan, after you went running straight into the arms of my best friend."

"I was so stupid," her voice cracked. She would not allow herself to cry in front of James, never again. "So stupid to ever get involved with you, I should have known that I couldn't trust you, that you would end up hurting me in the cruellest of ways, more than anyone else ever could have," she drew a deep breath. "Matthew was seeing me as a doctor. I'm pregnant," she stated, her voice devoid of any emotion.

CHAPTER FIFTEEN

"Meghan." James thought he may very well be about to be ill. He looked at the woman standing opposite him, her arms wrapped tightly around her middle as if to hold herself together. She was pregnant, and she had gone to Matthew for help instead of him. She didn't confide in him because she didn't trust him. Staring across at her, James watched as every one of his hopes and dreams incinerated, she would never forgive him for this. Even if they had been able to move on from the Jessinta issue, even if she had allowed him to explain, James knew that Meghan would never forgive him for accusing her of having an affair. He had been beyond cruel with his jealous accusations, and he was teetering on the edge of losing the only woman that he had ever really loved. "Meghan, I love you," he spoke through his tightening throat, feeling the magnitude of his loss, trying to clutch at anything to stop himself from drowning. She said nothing, just stared at him with sad eyes, unblinking, before giving a single nod.

"Don't ever talk to me again," her voice broke, a huge sob breaking free from deep inside of her, "I...hate...you," she whispered brokenly, "I hate you."

And just like that James was drowning, stumbling forward on unsteady legs, determined to reach Meghan, to make her see, to listen.

"James!" His sister's voice reached him from the doorway, her voice verging on hysteria. "James, mum...mum!" She held the doorframe for support, collapsing onto the floor, arm pointed towards the main house. James took off running, all thoughts of Meghan pushed from his mind, convinced by his sister's tone that he would arrive at the house to find his mother had passed away. Instead, he found her collapsed in the middle of the lounge room floor, Xavier and Matthew frantically performing CPR.

"What happened?" He ordered, dropping to his knees next to Xavier and Matthew.

"She saw me leaving your cottage this morning," Jessinta started, "when I came in to return my cottage key we got into an argument and she collapsed," she finished, wringing her hands together nervously. "I'm sorry, this is all my fault." Ignoring her, James watched as Xavier and Matthew worked, knowing that he could trust them with his mother's life, literally, that if they were unable to save her that it would not be for a lack of trying or of skill. James was vaguely aware that Meghan had joined the group of onlookers, that she had her arm around Arabella, holding her up.

"I have a pulse!" Matthew shouted, rolling Zonja into the recovery position as her eyes fluttered open. James hadn't realised he had been shaking until he went to clap his friends on their shoulders, unable to find the words required to thank them. They knew what he meant to say and were relieved that the outcome had been as happy as it had been, unwilling and incapable of even considering the alternative, not for James's mother, for Zonja who treated them as two more sons.

"Dad," James addressed his father, his voice of authority snapping his father out of his numbness. "I need you to call the Royal Flying Doctor Service, give them my name, tell them we need an aircraft here as soon as possible. Let them know I will be riding back with her, so they only need to send a flight nurse." His father nodded.

"Wait, James," Jessinta interjected. "I'll fly back with you, that way they can dispatch a plane right away, it will save time we may not otherwise have." James gave her a long hard look, nodding, she was right. "Dad tell them we just need a plane." His father went for the phone, too worried to argue.

"Are you out of your mind?" Arabella rounded on James. "Are you actually going to let her go with you? After she nearly killed mum?"

"Arabella, she's a trained flight nurse, it makes sense," James stated simply, not prepared to argue with his sister when she was obviously upset.

"No," Arabella refused to back down, "she is the reason mum has to go to the hospital in the first place."

"Arabella, please, don't. It is not Jessinta's fault," Meghan spoke softly, her voice dignified. James looked at her flabbergasted, was she actually defending Jessinta? The room fell quiet, aware of the undercurrent but not quite sure what to do about it.

"How can you say that, how can you defend her, you know what she did." Arabella stood, mouth gaping open. "I heard you and James fighting, she ruined everything!"

"Arabella," Meghan started, attempting to draw her into her outstretched arms.

"No," Arabella pushed Meghan's arms away. "I don't believe you. How can you say that, how? You love my brother, you do, I know you do. You're pregnant!" Arabella was screaming now, hysterical, unable to fathom what Meghan was saying. "You are supposed to be happy, and now she comes along and snaps her fingers and he runs back to her, like a dog!" Years of repressed rage spilled forth, poisoning her words.

"Like a dog, so that she can whip him again until he is cowed and broken. Then she'll just throw him away like trash," Arabella gasped for breath. "She nearly destroyed him last time, Meghan, you don't know, you didn't see, but we did. We thought he would never be himself again, never trust anyone else to get close to him, and then you came along. You are two halves of a whole, we all saw it, you belong together. That's why mum collapsed, she couldn't bear to see him throw it all away on her, couldn't bear to see it happen again." Arabella fell to the floor, sobbing. The room watched, shell-shocked. They had no idea that Arabella had carried this anger and bitterness with her for so long. All of his sisters were now crying, their husbands quietly moving the kids away from the room, through to their respective bedrooms. Meghan looked completely numb, moving to sit next to Arabella on the floor, and drawing her sobbing frame upwards, resting her head in her lap, stroking her hair, until her tears abated.

"Arabella, you can't help who you love." Meghan looked at James and Jessinta, the cause of so much anguish, seeing them for the first time. "No matter how painful it is or how much hurt it causes."

"I know, but you..." Arabella let the sentence hang, not sure how she wanted it to end.

"Arabella, in the grand scheme of things I am inconsequential," there was no spite in Meghan's voice, James realised that she actually believed what it was that she was saying. "The Royal Flying Doctor Service aircraft will be here soon, you have to let James do his job, trust him, he knows what needs to happen from now on." Arabella nodded, too tired to keep arguing. "We should go and help everyone else, the children are probably scared, and we need to get the cars packed with whatever essentials you think you'll need in order to stay in Alice Springs while your mum recovers." Meghan stood, helping Arabella up and leading her from the room, not even glancing in James's direction, feeling too raw and hollow to acknowledge him.

They found the children rather subdued, busy packing a small backpack each, older ones helping the younger ones with shoes and jackets. Leaving Arabella to supervise them, Meghan wandered through to the kitchen, hunting around until she had located some cooler bags and thermoses, busying herself with making drinks and sandwiches, and packing as much food into each cooler bag as she could.

Meghan placed the cooler bags and thermoses on the front porch, adding a box of non-perishable food to the pile, sure that it would be appreciated once the family arrived in Alice Springs. Meghan doubted that anyone would be wanting to go to the shop for a few days. She stepped to one side as she heard voices headed towards her, James, Matthew, Xavier and Gerhardus carrying Zonja out on a hard-plastic stretcher, no doubt kept on the property to assist injured people to the runway, followed closely by Jessinta. As Meghan watched them load the stretcher onto the back of a farm ute, she moved forward. "Jessinta, wait." Every muscle in James's body tensed, he knew his surprise was mirrored in everyone else's faces. "Here," Meghan thrust a small cooler bag and two thermos mugs of steaming hot coffee towards her. "No one ate much at breakfast today, this should tide you both over until you get home," her voice felt raw as she said the word home. Something she would never have, not anymore. Unable to watch James leaving her for the last time, she turned and walked away, head held high.

"Thank you," Jessinta called to Meghan's retreating back.

Meghan finished her packing, fingering her moonstone necklace one last time before placing it in the middle of James's bed. She wheeled her suitcase back to the main house and left it with the others. Everyone else had now packed a small case or bag with their necessities and were packing cars and corralling children. They would leave the bulk of their belongings here and had decided to carpool as much as possible into Alice Springs, not knowing what the parking would be like when they arrived there. Matthew, Xavier and Gerhardus arrived back at the house, helping to swap over car seats and locking up the house. No one spoke to Meghan, a fact she was grateful for. Perching on the front veranda, Meghan heard the sound of a small aircraft and looked up, seeing the Royal Flying Doctor Service plane passing overhead, with a waggle of the wings. She watched it until it was only a speck in the clear blue sky, not even bothering to try and hide the tears that coursed down her cheeks.

CHAPTER SIXTEEN

"Matthew, stop!" Pulling off the road in a cloud of dust, Meghan flung open the car door and scrambled out, staggering across to the closest bush before throwing up. This was the third stop that they had had to make, and they had not even made it to the small town of Ti Tree yet. Each stop was worse than the last, Meghan becoming more and more withdrawn and dehydrated the closer they got to Alice Springs. Not wanting to be social or pretend to understand what had happened, she had turned down invitations from James's sisters to travel back to Alice Springs with them, opting instead to go with Matthew, Xavier and Gerhardus, who she knew would be too preoccupied with their own thoughts to bother her. She had sat, rigid, in the back of Matthew's car, arms wrapped tightly around herself, lips pressed together, unwilling to enter into any form of conversation. Xavier had sat beside her, throwing worried glances her way, trying not to let her see.

As they left the town of Tennant Creek, images had flooded Meghan's mind, of James making love to her, the way he called her exquisite and swore that he was over Jessinta. The images wouldn't stop, it was as if a tap had been turned on, and bile rose up in Meghan's throat, threatening to choke her. She had asked Matthew to stop the car, had been violently ill until she was shaking all over, and still the images burned behind her eyes. She had dropped to her knees and sobbed until she was gasping for breath, ignoring Xavier's offered bottle of water, and refusing Matthew's offer to sit in the front seat. The second stop was less dramatic than the first, brought on with Gerhardus chatting out loud about James, having never before had reason to see him in doctor mode, and understandably proud at what he had witnessed. This time they had overruled Meghan's protests, and had installed her in the front seat in the hopes that it might help to settle her stomach down.

After this third delay, Matthew had pushed a bottle of water into her hand and told her to drink it, doctor's orders, that becoming dehydrated and ending up in hospital was not something that anyone wanted to see happen. Meghan drank it dutifully, then closed her eyes, and finally dozed off, grateful for the reprieve. Meghan's constant bouts of sickness had meant that they were pulling into the Alice Springs hospital carpark far later than they had originally intended, the rest of the family already there, James's sisters outside waiting for Gerhardus to arrive, their husbands having already secured a hotel room for them for the night, the children having been taken straight there to be fed and put into bed. "Dad!" Arabella rushed forward, engulfing Gerhardus in a hug. "Mum is going to be fine, James says she probably won't even need to be transported down to Adelaide. He's up there with her now, she's on the surgical ward, we can go straight through." As Gerhardus, Matthew and Xavier moved to follow Arabella, Meghan hung back by the car, her suitcase at her feet. "Meghan?" Arabella spoke. "Aren't you coming too? I know that mum and James are looking forward to seeing you."

"No, you go ahead," her voice sounded tired, defeated. "This is a time for family, not for work colleagues."

"What?" Gerhardus was puzzled. "You are family."

"Gerhardus, thank you," Meghan placed a kiss on his weathered cheek. "I appreciate you saying that, but we both know that I am not a part of your family. I hope Zonja is okay, I really do. If there is anything that you need, any of you, while you are in Alice Springs, just go to the switchboard and ask them to call me. Matthew can show you where it is on your way past, you will walk straight past it now in fact," she looked to Matthew who nodded his head. "I will miss you all," she coughed to try and hide the fact that her voice was at breaking point, "more than you will ever know." She looked around at the little group, gave them a wobbly smile and a nod, then turned her back and walked away. Once out of sight, Meghan fished her mobile phone out of her bag and called Tessa, asking her to please come and pick her up. While she waited for Tessa, Meghan flipped through her phone contacts list, navigating to James's number, and staring at it, her finger hovering over the delete button. Tessa's car horn startled Meghan out of her trance, and she hit the delete button and threw her phone back in her bag.

Meghan was overwhelmed with gratefulness to be back in her own little home. Tessa had taken one look at Meghan, hugged her tightly, and then not uttered a word. Meghan left her suitcase in the corner of the lounge room, too tired to even think about sorting through it right now. Tessa was on a day shift tomorrow and so took herself to bed, telling Meghan to come and get her if she needed to talk about anything, Meghan promised that she would. Taking the phone off the hook, Meghan ran a bath and filled it with the scented bubbles that Tessa had given her for Christmas, sinking into the luxurious warmth, letting all of the stress and worry slip away. She rested her hand on her flat stomach. It was hard to imagine that in less than nine months she would be a mother, a thought that terrified her. She didn't know the first thing about being a mother, about looking after a child of her own. There was so much that Meghan would need to work out. How would she possibly be able to keep working a shift work job with a child? How could she possibly afford not to work? There was no way that she would be taking anything from James, or any of his family either, of that she was already certain. Meghan had hoped that her bath would help her relax enough to fall asleep, but sleep eluded her, her head too busy with thoughts of her uncertain future.

Giving up on any idea of sleep, Meghan got out of bed and dressed, scrawling a note on a piece of paper for Tessa, leaving it on the kettle for her to find should she wake up and worry. Picking up Tessa's car keys from the bookcase near the front door, Meghan slipped out of the house as quietly as she could, winding the window down all the way, enjoying the feel of the night air blowing across her face, clearing the cobwebs from her mind. She drove the short distance to the Alice Springs hospital, easily finding a spot in the staff carpark. Using the back entrance, not wanting to answer any questions from the skeleton staff that worked around the switchboard office as to why she was back in Alice Springs, in the hospital, in the middle of the night, when she should still be away, Meghan took the stairs up to the second floor. No one batted an eye when Meghan walked through the doors of the surgical ward, holding her staff pass up just in case someone should want to see it. She located Zonja's name on the patient board, then walked down the corridor and slipped through the door, relieved to find her alone in the room, her family having already left. Meghan crossed to Zonja's bed, satisfied to see her in person, looking a lot better than she had the last time Meghan had seen her.

Meghan moved to the visitor chair placed next to the bed and sat, taking Zonja's hand in her own. She wondered if Zonja could hear her, if she knew that she was even here with her. "Zonja, it's Meghan," she kept her voice low, bending over to speak close to Zonja's ear. "We are all back in Alice Springs, did you know that? I can't stay long, it is the middle of the night, and I am pretty sure that I would be thrown out if anyone saw me here," Meghan chuckled at the thought of the staff calling down to the switchboard and getting them to page security to remove her. She would never live it down. "I just wanted to see you, to tell you thank you for having me for your anniversary celebrations. I am sorry for how it all ended, but I am not at all sorry that I came in the first place. I will never regret knowing you, any of you." Meghan squeezed Zonja's hand. "I don't know if anyone has told you yet, but I am pregnant. You are going to have another grandchild, at least I hope you will," uncertainty coloured Meghan's voice, "I would like you to be involved in their life, physically I mean, obviously not financially, I am not asking for any money or support, I just…Thought it would be nice if one day they can know their extended family."

"Meghan?" Jerking her head up, Meghan saw Gerhardus standing in the doorway.

"Gerhardus! How long have you been standing there?"

"Long enough. My son may not know what is good for him, but we do. You are a part of this family, Meghan, and we don't intend on ever letting you go, either of you." Gerhardus smiled.

Meghan shifted awkwardly, "Gerhardus, please don't tell anyone I was here, I don't want them knowing. This is a very small hospital and gossip spreads like wildfire," Meghan elaborated.

"I won't, I promise", he studied her thoughtfully. "Meghan, whatever happens, Zonja and I will be thrilled to welcome another grandchild. If you need anything, please come to us." Meghan nodded that she would. "Please keep in touch with us?" Gerhardus asked.

"I will," Meghan stated, standing and crossing the room. "I better go, you never know who is lurking in the hallways," she joked, hugging Gerhardus goodbye.

Gerhardus stared at his son as he strode into the room, an air of authority cloaking him. "Dad, I will be here with mum, why don't you go back to my unit, you can have a shower and something to eat, maybe even a rest." James urged.

"No." Gerhardus looked at his son. "It is you who should be leaving."

"I told you, dad, it isn't a problem, I am still on leave for a few more days, and I can always take more time off if need to, it is fine." James sighed. He had had this exact same conversation with his dad half a dozen times already and was growing weary of it. He didn't want to be in his unit by himself, not without Meghan, everywhere he looked he was reminded of her.

"That is not what I meant, James. I am talking about Meghan."

"Dad," James warned, he was not in the mood to discuss this with his dad.

"No, you listen to me. You need to fix this, James, before it is too late."

"Dad," James growled, "enough!"

"She is pregnant for goodness sake! She is carrying your baby, yours! Don't you feel anything for her?" Gerhardus snarled at James.

James looked at his dad incredulously. "Yes dad, as it happens, I love her, okay, but I screwed it all up, all of it, and now," he shrugged his shoulders helplessly, "I have lost everything I ever wanted."

Gerhardus glared at James. "James, you are my son and I love you, but sometimes you are an idiot." Gerhardus shook his head sadly. "Have you tried telling Meghan that you are sorry, that you love her?"

"She won't listen to me dad, I really hurt her," of this James was certain.

"Then you make her listen. James, if you don't at least try to fix this thing between you and Meghan, you will regret it for the rest of your life, and I think that you know that is true. You need to tell her the truth, all of it, no matter how much it hurts you to do so. Leave nothing out, if you are going to fix this James, you need to be completely honest with her."

"And if that doesn't work? If she can't forgive me, dad, what then?"

"Then that is something that you will need to learn to live with. It has to be her decision James, you can't rush it, give her enough space to come to a decision if she needs it. Honestly though, James," Gerhardus shook his head at his son's obvious blindness, "she loves you. A love like that doesn't just die."

"She said she hated me," James confessed.

"What would you expect her to say? She is trying to save face. If she didn't love you James she wouldn't be so bereft, so upset with you. I have only ever seen that level of grief once before in my life, and that was when your grandmother lost her husband. Now, shut the door on your way out, I'm going to have a short kip until your mother wakes up." James knew that his father was most probably right, as he was with most things, and as much as it scared him, he knew what it was that he had to do now. Back in his unit, James hurried through his shower, dressing in jeans and a cotton tee shirt. He picked up the ring box sitting next to his bed and opened it, looking inside, his stomach churning. He snapped the lid shut, shoved it in his pocket, and headed out of the door.

CHAPTER SEVENTEEN

Meghan was still sleeping when Tessa went to go to work, opening the door just as James was about to knock on it, standing there with his fist raised.

"Tessa, hi, is she here?"

"Yup," Tessa stood firm, staring down at James.

"Please, Tessa, can I come in? I need to talk to her."

"She's asleep at the moment."

"I can wait quietly until she wakes up, please?" James begged. "I need to talk to her, it's important."

"I don't know what it was that you did to her James, but I have never seen her this way before. I have to go to work, if you say anything to upset her or hurt her even more than what she already hurts, I won't hesitate to make your working life a living hell, and don't think that I can't, I have friends who work at the bloody switchboard, they run the hospital." James nodded at Tessa to show he understood, impressed that such a gentle-looking woman could actually be so fierce. Tessa moved out of the doorway, allowing James inside, then fixed him with her steely gaze and left for work, wondering if she had in fact done the right thing.

James sat at the kitchen table, waiting, as the clock hands ticked further and further around the face. Shortly before noon, he heard Meghan stirring, and braced himself, ready to face her. "Hi." his strong voice resonated throughout the large kitchen, as Meghan walked in.

"What the? How did you get in here? Actually, never mind," she greeted him coolly, "get out of my house." She walked to the front door and threw it open.

"Meghan, please don't throw me out," James hated the desperation in his voice, but was helpless, he was at Meghan's mercy. "Please, I just want a chance to explain."

"Are you joking?" Meghan scoffed, "I owe you nothing." she spat.

"Please Meghan, I love you." She looked at him then, really looked at him.

"No James, you don't," her voice was wistfully sad. "If you did, you would never have slept with your ex-girlfriend. You would never have kissed her, and you would never have led me on."

"What? Meghan, I never led you on."

"You made me think...I told you things, about me, and you let me think it was all okay, but it wasn't, James. It never was. You lied to me!" Meghan brushed angrily at the tears falling down her face. "I hate you," she lied.

"I love you, Meghan, that is something that will never change."

"Stop saying that. Do you think I care? Do you think that I want to keep hearing you say that? Stop torturing me, please, just stop it!"

"Meghan," her name sounded scratchy as he pushed it through the lump that had formed in his throat, a prayer, a question, he was no longer sure. "Please don't cry, please, sweetheart, let me explain." She shook her head vigorously. "Meghan I never lied to you, not once, also, since we are apparently discussing what we are not going to discuss, I also never kissed Jessinta, nor did I sleep with her!" James reached out slowly and brushed a stray tear from Meghan's chin. "May I please explain everything to you? That is all I am asking Meghan. Just sit down and listen to me, and then I promise that I will go."

"And never contact me again?" Meghan pressed, the request killing her a little bit on the inside. It is for the best she reasoned with herself, once she knew the truth, she would never want to see him again, of that she was sure.

"Meghan, I..." How could he possibly agree to that? Yet how could he not? He had to get her to listen to him, and if this was the only way, he had to do it. "Okay, Meghan. If you listen to me, and then you still want me to leave, I will. And I will never contact you again."

Sitting at the small table across from Meghan seemed like the strangest case of de je vu to James, and he took a moment to sort through his thoughts before he began. He wished he knew what Meghan was thinking, how she was feeling, but he suspected any enquiries into her health would not be welcomed from him. "When Jessinta showed up at my parent's property I was as stunned as everyone else. I was also...Conflicted," he searched for the right word. "I had planned the perfect day for us, the day I admitted my feelings to you, and in she storms, bringing nothing but chaos and irritation," he paused. "I couldn't throw her out Meg, regardless of who she was or what she had done in the past, I could not have thrown her out."

"I know," Meghan agreed with him, James would never turn someone out unless they had somewhere else to go.

"When I took her to her cottage, she told me that she had come all this way so that she could talk to me. I refused to listen. Then, when we were playing charades, she told me it was important, it was about the research she had stolen from me." James stopped talking and moved to get a glass of water, bringing one back for Meghan.

"Why didn't you tell me?" Meghan pressed. "I saw how you leant into her, how she," Meghan could barely stand to say it, "touched you at lunch!" Meghan choked out.

"I'm so sorry Meg, I knew that you would be jealous, but I had honestly thought that I would have time to explain it all to you later."

"In any case," James continued, "she only did that to annoy my sisters, they always had a fractious relationship. So, I went with her, back to her cottage, to hear her out. She apologised, Meg," James sounded stunned. He still couldn't quite believe it. "She owned up to the medical board about her plagiarism, they have stripped her of all recognition, and have republished the research and paper under my name, apparently they have sent a copy on to me."

"That's good," Meghan commented, "I'm glad you finally got the credit that you deserve."

"That is where we left it, Meg. I returned to my cottage and she stayed in hers. I didn't go back to the main house because I wasn't prepared to have to explain it all to anybody until I had explained it to you, but when I knocked on your door there was no answer, you must have already been asleep."

"Possibly, I had an early night, I wasn't feeling well."

"Then at breakfast...Meg, I have never felt so broken as I did sitting next to you that day. It felt as if there was a gulf between us, I didn't know how to reach you," he confessed. "And then," he swallowed hard, determined not to leave anything out, "I went to find you when you were sick, and I overheard you and Matthew talking, well, some of your conversation anyway. I was gutted, I thought..." he couldn't say it.

"You thought that I was having an affair, cheating on you with your best friend." Meghan supplied for him. "Do you really think that little of me?"

"I didn't know what to think, Meg, I was unsettled with Jessinta in the house, and I let my imagination get the better of me. I thought I was overhearing a conversation between lovers, and I was jealous. I should have confronted you instead of escaping back to my cottage."

"And kissing Jessinta," Meghan whispered.

"No!" James vehemently denied her allegation. "It was not like that Meg, I swear to you. I was there, stewing about what I had overheard between you and Matthew when Jessinta arrived. She told me again how very sorry she was, and I forgave her. She asked me if there was any possibility that we could ever have another shot at our relationship, that she still wanted me." James shifted uncomfortably. "That I didn't have to settle, that I could have her back if I wanted to."

"Oh," Meghan really didn't know what to say to that.

"So, you see Meg, it was a goodbye kiss, one that was very much only one-sided." James grinned at her obvious confusion.

"I don't understand, she said you could have her back."

"She did. The thing is Meg, I don't want her back, which is what I told her. This time, I am not going to settle, this time I am not accepting anything less than love. Real," James stood, "forever," he walked around to Meghan's chair, "until death we do part," he took her hands in his, "love."

He cupped her face then, his thumbs brushing away her tears. "It is you I want Meg, you who completes me, you who makes me want to be a better man, you that I love."

"You love me?" Meghan could not believe what she was hearing.

"Yes." James laughed. "I love you, Meg," he kissed her gently, "I love you, forever."

"I don't really hate you," Meghan sobbed, "I just said that to be mean." James held her as she cried, telling her that everything would be okay, that nothing else mattered except that they were together. After her tears had subsided, James carried her through to the bedroom, and undressed her with reverence, kneeling to feather kisses across her still flat stomach, gathering her close to him, marvelling that his child, their expression of love, was nestled in there, contentedly growing. Meghan reached down and tugged at his shirt, and he laughingly moved his arms from around her waist, standing up and stripping his clothes off, gathering her back in his arms and placing her carefully on the bed as if she were made of glass. Meghan smiled up at James from between her lashes, his gaze raking over her body, drinking her in, committing her to memory. Slowly, very slowly, he leant down, capturing Meghan's mouth in a kiss that was so full of love and promise, that it left her in doubt as to his feelings for her.

James's hand slid down, gliding over Meghan's stomach and down further, to cup her centre, growing hard at the discovery of her wetness, idly wondering if the day would ever come when he would tire of knowing that he made her that wet. With a sigh of contentment, he dipped his head to capture her breast, teasing her nipple until he felt it harden and pebble beneath his tongue, suckling and biting, loving the sounds it elicited from Meghan. His fingers slipped further down, delving into her silky folds, dipping in and out with a leisurely speed, as Meghan moaned and writhed beneath him. Releasing her swollen nipple, James moved his attentions lower still, probing his tongue into her very core, teasing, tasting, drinking in her juices, as she bucked her hips beneath him, her breathing growing laboured. Rising to his knees, James spread her knees even further apart, wanting to see all of her, loving the sight of having her open for him, knowing that she was his alone. He lent over her, driving his erection into her, before pulling out fully and driving in again. Meghan arched her back and bucked her hips to meet his powerful thrusts, screaming in pleasure as he drove in harder and deeper, his thick member filling her to breaking point, his pelvic bone pressing against her sensitive nub. Meghan held nothing back as he moved within her, she was his completely. Pulling his length out fully, he gave one final thrust all the way into her core and felt her walls tighten around his stiffened member as he pushed her over the edge, hearing her scream out his name with wild abandon. With one final thrust he exploded inside her, gripping her hips for support, until totally spent, he collapsed beside her.

"Meghan," James shifted, reaching onto the floor to collect his pants, fishing around in his pockets until he found what he was looking for, turning back to Meghan and offering her an open ring box. "I have loved you since your night in the bush, I have loved you since before you gave me the greatest gift of all," he touched her stomach lovingly. "This ring was my grandmother's, my father pulled it out of the family safe the night of your bush adventure. I know that you said you would never marry, but I think I can persuade you," he smiled and dipped his head, kissing her stomach, moving slowly upwards. "Marry me Meg? Trust me to take care of you, both of you. Take a chance on me, on us, and I will spend the rest of my life showing you just how much I love you. Will you marry me?" He slid the ring, a moonstone and diamond creation, onto her finger.

"Yes," the word was barely a whisper, yet carried to James as if it had been shouted. Meghan melted into James as his mouth claimed hers, certain in the knowledge that this is where she was supposed to be.

As the car crawled to a stop, Meghan gasped, blinking rapidly in an attempt to keep her tears at bay. The scene that greeted her was breathtaking. The men in the family had been busy the past few days, aided by Xavier and Matthew, who had both told Meghan on several occasions just how happy they were for her and James. Trees had been felled and fashioned into rustic wooden pews, arranged in a semi-circle around the clearing in which Meghan had first known she had loved James, the night that he had saved her from being lost. Hundreds of strands of fairy lights had been strung up in the gum trees, and an aisle of tea light candles stretched from where James was nervously waiting to where Meghan's car had stopped, adding a special glow to their twilight ceremony.

Gerhardus walked around and opened Meghan's door, offering his arm as she stepped out. Tessa and James's sisters all joined her, fussing around with straightening Meghan's dress, a classic Grace Kelly inspired design that she had taken immense joy in making herself, with a little help from her future sister, Arabella, the two becoming almost inseparable. Tessa smiled at Meghan, and once satisfied that everything was in order, she handed over Meghan's bouquet, a stunning mixture of wildflowers that the women in James's family had taken great delight in helping her to pick this morning over a surprise picnic breakfast. Tessa nodded at the flautist, who began playing "You Are The Reason" by Calum Scott, and moved to the start of the aisle where she began sending children off down the aisle, every one of James's nieces and nephews having been promised a role in their wedding party, looking adorable in miniature versions of James's and Meghan's wedding clothes. Once the last child had been sent down the aisle, Gerhardus and Meghan took their places, and with a nod from Tessa, the flautist began the bridal march, Meghan and Gerhardus stepping out to start their journey.

Meghan couldn't keep her eyes off James, she could hardly believe that he was actually hers, that she was about to marry him, to be Mrs Cristo. If it had not been for Gerhardus walking next to her, keeping her walk at a snail's pace, Meghan would have run down the aisle, a fact that James delighted in realising. Flanked by Xavier and Matthew, James was dressed in a jet-black tuxedo, having declared to Meghan that in no uncertain terms would he be wearing jeans to their wedding, no matter how sexy she found them to be on him, that when he married her, he intended to do it in style. She had kissed him thoroughly and told him that as long as he showed up, he could wear whatever he wanted to.

As Meghan drew closer to the alter, she looked around at all of the people who had come so far to celebrate their day. It seemed as if everyone who had been able to get the time off had come, even some friends who were currently working overseas had found the time to come. Meghan recognised quite a few people that James worked with from the Alice Springs hospital, having extended his contract indefinitely in order to be closer to his family, as well as some who she knew to be the Cristo neighbours and friends, all delighted to be included in their special day, thrilled to be able to share their congratulations. James's family took up all of the first three rows of pews, their tears and happy faces telling her how happy they were that this day was here at last, just as they had told her often in the past few months just how blessed they felt to have her join their family.

Right at the front pew was Zonja, beaming, proudly holding up her two newest grandsons, refusing all offers of help from others wishing to snuggle the babies. At just four months old, Oscar Xavier Cristo and Oliver Matthew Cristo, named for their doting Godfathers, had become two cooing bundles of perfect cuteness who had managed to completely wrap their entire family around their fingers. Meghan paused to kiss their chubby little cheeks before joining their daddy, her eyes full of love for this man who had given her everything that she never knew she had wanted. Standing in front of their family and friends, Meghan and James pledged to love, support, and encourage each other, until death do they part, a promise they kept for the rest of their days.

Much later, wrapped up in each other's arms beneath a canopy of trailing ivy leaves, Meghan placed James's hand on her stomach with a secret smile and told him that she suspected their family may be about to grow bigger. Eyes growing larger, James had crushed her to him, laughing with delight, rejoicing in just how very lucky he was.

THE END

If you enjoyed this, or any of my other novels, please consider leaving a review.

About The Author

An international bestselling and award-winning author of sweet contemporary romance, Kathleen's novels showcase thought provoking plots and strong emotions that have been likened to a Hallmark movie. Featuring feisty heroines and strong heroes, where everyone gets a happily ever after. To discover more about Kathleen: https://linktr.ee/KathleenRyder

Join Kathleen Online

Facebook[1]

Instagram[2]

BookBub[3]

Goodreads[4]

Read More of Kathleen's Books

Cinnamon Kisses and Gingerbread Wishes[5]

The Flying Doctor's Christmas Wish[6]

The Brooding Doctor's Christmas Wish[7]

Christmas Wish Collection[8]

The Surgeon's Baby[9]

Fling With The Flying Doctor[10]

The Marriage Deal[11]

Caleb's Song[12]

---

1. https://www.facebook.com/kathleenryderauthor/

2. https://instagram.com/kathleenryderauthor

3. https://www.bookbub.com/authors/kathleen-ryder

4. https://www.goodreads.com/author/show/20624972.Kathleen_Ryder

5. https://books2read.com/CinnamonKissesGingerbreadWishes

6. https://books2read.com/FlyingDrsChristmasWish

7. https://books2read.com/BroodingDrsChristmasWish

8. https://books2read.com/ChristmasWishCollection

9. https://books2read.com/SurgeonsBaby

10. https://books2read.com/FlingWithTheFlyingDr

11. https://books2read.com/MarriageDeal

12. https://books2read.com/CalebsSong